The
Honeyman Festival

Also by Marian Engel:
No Clouds of Glory

The
Honeyman Festival

A NOVEL BY MARIAN ENGEL

ST. MARTIN'S PRESS   NEW YORK

For Hana
who wrote to me from
Katmandu

1

Minn was in the bath, and filled the bath. The globe of her belly rose above the waterline to meet the spotted ceiling. She thought, it's going to be soon, or a very big kid. It won't hold on another six weeks. I won't stretch any farther, it's as far out as it was when the twins were in there.

Yesterday, when she got on the streetcar, she had had to heave herself up the step using her hands under her belly as a kind of sling. Towards the end, she thought, it's more a thing than a part of yourself. It ripples with a motion you did not cause. It is an appurtenance of the child, not quite your own body now.

Yet it was her own flesh, the whey-colour of the moon, livid Cranach-flesh, very delicate to look upon, the skin so stretched it divided itself into cells so that at last she believed in cells; thin enough, perhaps, to see through, if she had the will, the energy, to peer down, down, down to the child.

She ran more water, very hot water. To take the stickiness of the long day away.

At first Mordie had thought it was another pair of twins, and sent her for an x-ray, and found there was no danger of that. So it was going to be a very big baby, a boy she hoped for the sake of symmetry. Or perhaps they were a month out on the date. Because no matter what Mordie said it was not going to hang on until the 8th of June.

As the water rose around her, the child kicked and plunged. She tapped it gently with an extended finger, to let it know how things would be if she had the strength. From conception, there was a relationship of sorts. She covered her belly with a wrung-out washcloth to keep it warm.

Around her, the house was silent. It was only seven, but all three of them slept as if they had invented sleep, tongues and arms askew, bums in the air, blankets over their heads. Bennie twisted and floundered like a whale every night, heaving and knotting his fingers together over his head, reaching out for comforts in the dark. They had been out in the mud at the back all day. She would have to remember to worm them soon. And to put a load of washing in when she got out of the bathtub.

Half an hour ago, the so-called Flower Children she let the attic to had laid zithers, guitars and sitars aside and thundered out for pizza. Norman, as usual, was away. If that meant loneliness, it meant also that what was left of wakefulness was hers alone. She could hear time ticking around her, beginning to expand.

Just over four years ago, fertility had taken them by storm. Louisa made them happy, even being pregnant with Louisa made them happy; especially that, for they had wanted to make love all the time, and felt free to. So after Louisa was ambulant, they launched into what turned out to be Bennie and Til.

And, since condoms puncture, dutch caps fly greased into the furthest dusty corner of the bathroom on their coiled spring rims, pills reduce the libido and increase the protruding veins, this one was to be born wearing a Lippes Loop for a lorgnette in June. She was nearer forty than thirty.

He belted her again. Perhaps he was feeling the chill. She turned the hot on again with her soggy feet, and let it run until she was sweating and flushed. She washed her face and her arms languidly. She was very tired. You weren't supposed to take fat, hot baths in mausoleum tubs towards the end of a pregnancy, you were apt to fall asleep and drown or fall and break your neck getting out or grab the electric light to save yourself and be found blue, naked and rigid on the mat next day by a window-washer, or get Ajax up the birth canal. In some ways, life was comically reduced: sin a chocolate bar at a bus stop, adventure a forbidden bath.

She lay back, twisted her neck, considered herself. She was ugly, ugly and hairy with it; rippled with fat. Blue fingers of stretch-marks held up her belly. Later, they would fade to pale striations, silver tracks of glaciers or snails. And there would be there, again, the negroid pigmented line from navel to *mons*. Something primaeval and sinister about that, hidden where you could not crane to see it, your body pulling a fast one.

She wasn't, any more, in good shape. Her doctor, Mordie, wasn't glad to see her. He liked fertility, he had the joy in him when he probed a belly or yanked a baby out of one, but he was disgusted by women who were soft, out of shape. Yesterday he had not smiled when he listened to the heart, or joked over the fore-finger examination, or, knowing that Norman was away, flattered her sagging vanity. He said, "Why don't you do some work around the house for exercise?"

"It's soon, isn't it?"

"June the eighth, baby, June the eighth. Uncle Mordie's never wrong. You're eating too much, watch it."

There was beer in the afternoon after wiping the nap-shit off the walls, and peanut butter sandwiches when they got her up at night, and eating their leftovers, and guzzling and stuffing when you were too angry to consider hitting them. And you couldn't walk it off, you didn't have three hands, they took you along the street at a snail's pace, you idled, stooping to pick them up or put their

3

shoes on again or take the cigar butts away, you felt the flesh mounting and multiplying with frustration and knew that captivity was tolerable only when it was comfortable; you ate, you drank a little, you sat on the floor and rolled with them, indulged them, always tamping impatience down inside you, because it was their time now, not yours; you had had your adventures. But the spirit rebelled against their forced slow-march in little spurts and dangerous leaks. It was better to eat than to hit them even when they were naughty.

She was a little faint now, her head spun. Last night she had dreamed a dangerous dream. There was a sale of pyjamas at Eaton's, Doctor Dentons, fifty cents a pair. She took the housekeeping money and left the kids with the painters. She bought quantities of pyjamas which were new and unstretched and unfaded, had all their snaps: she rubbed her face on their fuzzy lining, felt morally quenched and found that what she had left of her money was a dollar ninety-eight. She left Eaton's by the Albert Street door to walk through the book department, and on a counter by that door there were emeralds, diamonds, Liberty silk scarves in paisley patterns, Eskimo carvings, and pieces of raw amber, each marked down to ninety-eight cents and no tax. She took a long, guilty time to choose.

The raw amber was most beautiful, the texture and colour of lemon soap. She thought she ought to prefer emeralds or diamonds, but there was the feel of the amber — and they couldn't have been good emeralds and diamonds, they were the size of golfballs and very roughly cut — she fingered silk, soapstone and amber, and thought, I have to go home, I'm late, and went on feeling. Because decisions of this moment had to be made carefully.

On the way home, she passed the fishmonger. The boy in the shop was wearing watercress in his Centennial straw hat. She knew that the painters left at noon, but she stayed and flirted with him, and bought sole and mussels and slices of swordfish and — wasn't it odd they sold it? — cream. She worried about the painters, but she had spent her bus money, and it was a fine day, she walked home.

4

When she burst in in her hurry, the house was silent. She found that she had put them to nap in the bath. They were beautiful, not puckered at all from the water. They were curled up like little gleaming fish, and dead.

Remembering the dream, her mouth was dry. This was the hardest instinct to face, the destructive one, when the sticky hands soiled the ego and the shrill demands plucked at the eardrums, and when you tried to steal a moment for yourself the innocent faces hardened into animal stupidity. Then you thought of Mrs-Prentice-in-Godwin who killed all hers with an axe (but not until after she had given Alice the blue flowered cream-and-sugar), and Prue Jarvis, who went to bed for a nap when her husband was in East Africa and woke a fortnight later in a psychiatric ward (not having committed violence, only neglect); and the small, sadistic gestures of women in imprisoned situations.

Norman was out most nights when he was not away. She had no family to help her, but she tried to arrange her life sensibly. One afternoon a week to wander, if she could find a sitter, one evening out, a movie when she was up-tight, and now, Jane-Regina, her mental health visitor. Still, she was shocked when the rough beast assaulted her dreams, the deep, selfish and murderous desire to be alone and independent again. She thought of visiting Prue in the hospital, who told her she had achingly empty arms: you only think you want to be alone, dear. She thought of Mrs Prentice locked away in Penetang and Mr Prentice slouching down Main Street with his piano-tuner's case of memories; of mothers and children locked together in Scarborough for the winter, the flakes of paranoia in the air: and the adults wondering why the children wanted to change the world. And Bertrand Russell saying, "Of course women's lives have improved; you simply, a hundred years ago, had a baby a year until you died of it."

She read a lot. They didn't like you to read, they felt rejected, they pestered, but she went on reading. She locked herself behind the bathroom door and them behind their gate and read for an hour every morning. She read a lot of novels and marvelled at the mass of dead children. Novelists could not resist dead children: Edna O'Brien, Durrell, Dickens, oh, Huxley and Waugh, Joyce even (the stillborn son of Bloom, that was): sweet corpses fell on fiction like leaves.

She bought paperbacks out of the housekeeping money. In the past year there had been several purported memoirs of youngsters who killed Mum with the axe. She could see why they'd want to, but it was the reverse that interested her. But nobody would want to feel through those emotions while making the fiction.

The Babes in the Wood was a good one: a delegated job, at that. The kind birds covering them up. Louisa liked it.

The kids had dark round heads like Norman's, and thick white necks. Today, even with the smell of spring in the air, even with robins singing and one-half a stunted daffodil blooming beside the steps, they had been subdued and virtuous and lovable. They had not, as they had yesterday, pelted her with turds in the morning, or kicked her belly and screamed in the evening, or thrown shoes out the window into the rain. Tonight she had a little strength left. And none of the things she had to do for later weighed heavily on her.

Sometimes, at this hour, she went to bed for a while. And got up later to watch old movies. She missed the queuing and the collectivity of going out to them, but when tickets were over two dollars and there was the sitter to pay it was seldom worth it, unless there was a director she was interested in.

Funny, before she went to France she hadn't known that films had directors the way books have authors. You learned a lot, growing up in a place like Godwin and moving on to a provincial university; you learned a lot, say, about the dear old nineteenth century. But not that films have directors.

She yawned again. She was having bouts of insomnia now, she was hopelessly sleepy until she went to bed.

6

Stayed up last night watching *Stella Nova*, shouldn't have. Wanted to hear Norman's voice again. It was good work, dubbing, putting on your mid-Atlantic accent and getting paid for it. My timing was out, as usual. Voice deeper than I remembered or imagined. Shrill now: YOU KIDS GET OUT OF THAT FRIDGE DO YOU HEAR ME? She resisted again the temptation to fall asleep in the bath. She stared hard at the flaking ceiling, looking for cracks like rabbits. There was an egg-and-dart moulding right around the room. It was a grand house once. Like the moulding on the old buildings up and down Spadina, made of pressed tin, now dripping and draping, rusty. The grandeur that was imitation Greece. Spacious ideas they had, then.

The house was spacious. She wondered if she would ever be able to move neatly through a sane-sized one, live without possessions scattered through fourteen crumbling rooms.

Fourteen rooms on a Thursday evening. You could go round and genuflect to all of them, as if they were stations of the cross. They were stations of the cross. She could not get over the fact that she was in charge of all of them, that when the plaster slid down and sat in a heap, or the bugs found a new place to proliferate, or the wiring protruded suddenly, it was hers to remedy the error. It took her weeks to realise that what they had in the ceilings was not a sprinkler system but a network of gas-jets, some of which were live. She had not expected to live this kind of life.

Oh, she had been warned. In Godwin, the upbringing of women was severely practical. But somehow it had not penetrated to her that frills and wax-looking dolls would lead to the coarse mysteries of pubic hair and blood in the pants and absent husbands, and that if they did, and she did not like it, she would be unable to take her Victorian self up to her room for 40 years. Enough of us go to asylums, she thought and remembered her mother Gertrude standing over her saying she had got to learn to scrub a decent toilet, and herself rebelling "Never!"; and the strength of Gertrude, her big feet; and her own angry tears. And that goddamn Gertrude accusing her of being finicky when the tears were for missing the swimming meet.

7

Though certainly there had been finickiness in her, a stiff *pudeur*. A failure to understand that part of life was properly Rabelaisian.

How could you teach that? Even the words were terrible. Bag of waters. Plug of mucus. What I harbour now. Is there an attitude I can teach the girls to take?

Keep them from shyness, keep them from snickering. They will end strapped on a table in a delivery room, their hands tied to the bed-sides. Bodies in two halves, sheets above and stirrups below; at the head an anaesthetist telling clinical jokes; at the waist, men working. Their privates sealed off and shaved and sterilised, delegated to professionals. The men will work well, and tell them it's for the good of the child, but something . . .

"He plunged his cock into my womb" . . . Annabel and I stealing the dirty note from the gaggle of marriageable grade-eighters, and never able to forget it. It had at the same time everything and nothing to do with our lives.

And Ben, last month, reached shyly up and touched me, murmuring softly, "Fur, fur." That made it all right again, when nothing before helped.

Her head sank, as it often did these days: sitting in the kitchen, peeling potatoes, even stirring eggs on the gas; bloodstream was occupied elsewhere than the brain. Or was the small parasite supping, gathering its strength for the voyage out? Psyche struggled against consciousness, she pulled the plug out with her toe, and braced herself against drowning, and slid into sleep.

And woke, suddenly, laughing.

Only the ghost, the outline of a dream, but good, guilty. Herself and Norman slippery on the landing, struggling in it, white, viscous and foaming stuff, the Mr Bubble of adults, colliding body-to-body in it like Turkish wrestlers, fighting, hurrying. Steps on the stairs, and "Coming" they yelled in unison but did not retreat, they were too much enjoying it, slip, slide, cling, roll in the seal-wallow, rubbing it into each other. Still it came bubbling out of him, fizzing. They clung, helpless, to each other. She laughed aloud and woke herself.

She inched herself out of the warm, smooth porcelain carefully, supporting her weight with shoulder muscles built by lifting large, solid children, and stood up, avoiding the sight of herself in the mirror. She covered herself inadequately in Norman's absorbent bathrobe, and padded down the corridor to her own room to dress, it was getting late, and there were things to do.

She resisted the temptation to fall asleep on the bed. She sat on the edge and her back hurt; she moved to the hard chair by the dressing table. She had a final feeling: she was all underparts and woollyheadedness, Mordie be damned. Her feet looked dangerously swollen. Perhaps she was only homesick for the maternity world: your five days' rest and your sitz bath and your enema; sunlamps and packed suitcases and, "Have your waters broken yet?" Open on a table to instruments, high on the epidural injection and enjoying it, but part of you wanting still to squat in a field and do it alone, though not with *placenta praevia*.

She stood up and rubbed Norman's imaginary lotion into her skin. Pity pregnancy made the libido sing and he was not here to enjoy it. Next time they send you away, they send us with you, fella. She put on one of his laundry-starched shirts and a pair of underpants so stretched they had no function except to be genteel. And house slippers and her pregnant flannel tent. Thursday evening. Jane-Regina coming. And at eleven, if she managed to stay awake, Mrs Norman Burge was kindly opening her spacious home on Bute Place to the celebrants of the closing night of the Honeyman Festival.

9

2

Knowing that Norman was to be so long away, knowing that women abandoned with infants are dangerous animals, and that with her friends she would be enduring the usual winter of frustrated sociability, she had schemed to make the city's social services work for her without actually being incarcerated by them. It was not easy.

She was not, like her Jane-Regina, dependent on days, on structured time; and most of the time she was happy to be alone. But she knew that she was as neurotic as most women, and that pregnancy in combination with isolation, pregnancy with a child who was not as welcome as the others had been, a pregnancy not socially acceptable in the days of anti-population crusades, with Norman on a journey that she longed to make herself, might break her slender strap of self-control. In addition to the arrival of the (thank god for, new, clean — and in a nylon net — virginal) diaper service, she needed one regular, independent adult event in her week. Failing a bridge club, a social worker seemed a good arrangement. Was it her fault if the agency she succeeded in convincing of her need sent her Jane-Regina Magill, the only girl she had absolutely hated in her life, the bitch-goddess of her year at boarding-school?

Hard enough to get Jane-Regina. A psychiatrist at a cocktail party told her that she ought not to complain: she spoke of three children as if they were forty, forgetting to mention that in her world she held absolute power: that had to be paid for. "Take it," she said, "take my power." Because the power was paid for every second in indecision; she knew that whatever she did to them or for them was forming them, and that their own natures were forming themselves in opposition to that power, and that the energy generated in the process was enough to destroy them all, and she fought against it.

The agencies she telephoned thought her peculiar. The psychiatrist suggested that she go out and do good works herself. Jane-Regina came through the good offices of the Junior League.

And what pleasure it gave Jane-Regina to come to the lonely, the defeated, the déclassé, to walk into the toweringly shabby house, leave her white kid boots on the unrecognizable scrap of Tabriz by the cracked hall window, scowl at the peeling bluebirds on the painted glass, and proceed warily, every inch a lady and bountiful to the core, into the drafty living room where Minn sat swathed in pregnancy and despair, no help, no money, wild raffish children — reaping where she had sown, lying in the bed she had unmade.

Minn went down the long steep staircase, caressing the sticky bannister, to the back kitchen to crush the ice for Jane-Regina's daiquiri. She put the ice in the freezer (once again moving the snowball she had put away in a plastic bag for Louisa) and went to tidy the living room, which belonged to their early, over-decorated period, when she had been clever with curtains and remnants and fringe, had had time to go to the sales and reconstruct the Victorian room: furniture collected annually from home, odd chairs and tables from the Salvation Army, half a dozen wicker plantstands containing dying aspidistras and ferns in the bay window; on the walls, articles associated with the lovers' game 'our past': a case of surgical instruments which had originally (gleaming in a midnight store window on the Boulevard St Germain) prompted them to go to bed, a row of covetable, childish wooden spoons a bad map of Paris and a good one of Alexandria, a Majolica plate, a Portobello photograph: nonsense, all, but pleasing. The upholstery would have been more impressive in velvet rather than corduroy, and the staples were showing badly.

She wiped the sticky edges of a marble card-table, looped the curtains back from the window and dusted the coffee table with the inside hem of her skirt. She turned

11

into the connecting dining-room and straightened the row of chairs. In the leather well of one of them someone had wet his pants. She went to get a duster to wipe it up, came back and thought, "God, how we used to spend our money!"

They rented the house from a woman who had hoped to turn it into a town house, but lost her money on the adjoining member of the row. They had taken it when Minn was pregnant with Louisa, full of the instinct to make a nest. It was an impossible house: drafty and bug-laden, lacking in storm windows and power-circuits, and imprac-tical for children; fourteen-foot high ceilings meant a long drop from upper windows (Norman had barred them all with half-round and a lack of interior doors meant a lack of privacy (Norman had bought all the expanding baby-gate at Salvation Army and the house was less a house than an obstacle-maze). She had many complaints about it: the registers belched soot, the yard was a mudhole of buried glass, the kitchen was freezing, she hated the bugs, the plumbing was always awry. But there were fourteen rooms and two of them were beautiful, the moulding in the hall was — it was only moulded plasterwork, but they didn't do that any more. Mordie said it was a shame to bring up kids in a house with stairs that dangerous, but Minn was the only one who had ever fallen down them.

Whether she liked the house or hated it depended on who had the upper hand that day, herself or the house. To its fourteen rooms it had two clothes-closets and a ten-dency to race out of control. Rubbish sat in humps about the long corridors, waiting to have decisions made: this was too heavy to move, that too precious to throw out. Benny and Til took this apart, Norman might one day fix it. They were downtown, in a night-collection area. Their garbage cans were stolen continually, the city would not remove anything unless it was in a can or a plastic bag. *The New York Times* piled up among legs of furniture and broken dolls. She was haunted by boxes and bags of miscellaneous objects and the thought that Norman did not like her to give a thing away. Whatever she packed up neatly, the children pounced on and unpacked. I ought, she thought, to borrow a week of Alice. She'd say "rubbish" and force me to throw half the house away. And envisaged the lot of them sprawled, bent, scraped and dusty, on a bulk-loader, the Burges headed like castoff toys for the dump.

She looked around the living room. It wasn't bad. The front half of the house had a kind of architectural grace that redeemed it from sordidness. In the back, where the function of the rooms had been determined by an older life-style, a different kind of furniture (the kitchen and back dining-room had once been crammed with storage pantries, portable larders, hutches, imitation armoires), their own disarray was confused and diffused. It was not like other people's houses.

It was the first time they had had a house of their own. Before, they had lived in innumerable hotel rooms, in lodgings, in furnished sublet flats, among objects they dared not impose their will upon. Now she stood still in front of her own taste and wondered, not for the first time, why she had made the house — with the help of the Salvation Army and Alice up home — so oddly theatrical. It was like a set, it expected a cast, klieg lights, a director and for ceilings the cord-wound rafters of an arena. People should come out of nowhere into this house, put on jobs and personalities, shout at each other . . .

She caught her breath. How Honeyman would . . . Laughed and stopped laughing. He was dead, God rest him, and out of her life long before that. Buried somewhere in the hills behind Cannes, and, as well, inside herself.

Honeyman. The name if she let it still causing sharp shooting sparks in the abdomen. Honeyman.

The great lolling length; body, as though partially disjointed, a lay figure, beside her; "Broke up", he said, from riding broncos, and scarred, certainly from the accident-prone days before she knew him, before she was born. The strange softness of the old-young drying skin, loose, a little loose, beginning to be liver-marked, but not pouchy. Exotic to her.

13

She sat, startled by waves of emotion. Years since she weakened last for him, though she had never stopped talking to him in her head, saying, "See, Honeyman?" when she did what she was proud of, or what he would like, or resisted him. And more often when she tried perversely to summon up his flesh it would be the firmer flesh of Norman burrowed into her that came to mind. And she loved Norman and the children, they were more to her, more hers, more real, more possible.

Only he was fifty-five to her twenty, and he knew a lot, and taught her some of it, it went in and stayed there and changed her in a direction she was thankful for. Friends murmured "father-figure" and she denied it, but he was, of course; a father chosen instead of imposed, who knew the things she wanted to know and taught her them.

What he gave me by knowing me. And I at twenty still wrapped in the cruel child's integument of innocence, insisting, demanding. Why didn't he throw me out or wring my sweet neck?

He was a kind man, he had patience, and children almost her age. When she lay beside him in bed and drew the heathen blanket of southern Ontario guilt around her, he turned to her, he comforted her, he talked to her, taught her what she was.

A strange man, long-headed, the grey hair curling high on the immense forehead, the nose falling straight to flared nostrils, the long upper lip, the wide, twisted thick-lipped mouth. Shooting sparks. A head on a grand scale, big-planed; and a body to match, bellyless, loose-jointed, Western and mythic in walk.

He was from Nebraska, the son of a wealthy cooper and a Christian Scientist. He had been sent to Princeton when he wanted to go further west. He left the university to take his kid's romanticism to California. Before he was twenty he arrived in Hollywood broken-backed. His father staked him to a second education in what he called "the pic-chahs".

Telling his story, leaving out the stress, the terrible passions of young-ness, lounging through it as if it were easy – he made everything look easy, even youth, Honey-man. He made it look easy to live, as if living were some road you strode along and not the puritan hurdle-course she had been taught to believe in.

And suddenly, because she knew him, it was easy: she had a flat in Paris when nobody had a flat in Paris, and jobs in films when nobody could break into films; when because of his terrifying American casualness and abrupt-ness nobody could make contact with him, she could. People looked at her enviously and asked why she was special. Even she, for a while, wondered why she was special. "You're not, kid," he said, "but I like you." She wondered at that, too, until she grew old enough to realise that if love is an accident, liking is a kind of miracle.

He liked her, he tried to make something of her. He like the way she looked, he said, the long legs, the big bosom, the way her lower lip stuck out. But he was not young any more, he told her that all she had to do was to be herself, and forgot that at her age even he had not discovered what to be that was himself; he was breaking horses with a background in Middle English. By the time she met him, he was as fixed and formed, it seemed to her, as she must seem to her upstairs hippies, a finished creation, no longer floundering in flux. Jesus; he thought the thing to do with Minn at twenty was teach her how to be un-self-conscious, and put her in his movies, it was that simple. And she went through terrors and uncertainties, wilting queasily before cameras, until they discovered that neither she nor God had dreamed she would become an actress.

Then he loosened his grip on her without dropping her. The liking continued. There were other jobs she could do, on the sets, in the studios. She picked up good French easily with the grammatical backing of years of drill-mistresses and *Cours Moyen*. Forty-two university term-papers had given her fluency in writing. She had been taught at home to make lists, to finish things. She had energy. She did not lose him.

In addition, he liked to eat with her. There were gilt and flashy ladies he took to the Tour d'Argent, and Minn

15

whom he took all over France snuffling out truffled patés and full-bodied wines and . . .

Honeyman. Years. Like some dreadful addiction, waiting for him as for a fix. Later, fighting him. "You're growing out of me," he said blandly, woundingly, almost relieved.

Honeyman. How fortunate to have . . . To have been sent to the cooking-school? To have spent the summer in Italy? Always alone in the flat in the rue Dragon. That was the arrangement, no visitors. Alone, knowing no one, waiting for him. Seeing no one for months when he was away, except the son, Cal, the rootless one, run away from another school and hiding out with a passel of rootless friends, destroying things, destroying himself.

Honeyman. My friends were marrying. How could they, not yet having turned into themselves? I waited. Finally, it was finished with him. Between sixty and twenty-five there is no democracy, I pushed for equality, I fought him fiercely, he married again.

The feeling, then: as if one's body is plaster, and flakes are falling, falling and one is finally to become the rusted, chipped maquette of a Giacometti.

She was not as young as she looked; she had money, she had class; she left her husband for him. She was in his circle. She had the villa for him to retire to. He was right.

After Norman and I got married I had cards printed, "Mme N. Burge," I dragged him down to Cannes, wrote on the inner fold, "Passons par Cannes et je me demande si c'est possible vous voir avant de partir pour l'Angleterre, Minn . . ." the name very large and determined. They were ladies and gentlemen: they telephoned at once, they sent their chauffeur to our ghastly hotel.

Minn heaving with nerves, swelling, sweating, her breasts pushing out in anguish, and Norman shrinking with embarrassment. Getting through the first Dubonnet without spilling. Honeyman his bland best, using his public manner. Minn knowing that. The blind intimacy pulled down. Liking the woman more.

On the way to the bathroom she faced Minn, Guinévre; she said, smiling, "So you have forgiven me!" Up close, she had crows' feet and a sense of humour. She had been a famous actress. The realisation that she was exactly right for Honeyman irked and ached.

In the salon (beams, and heavy English chairs and pottery from Moustiers) Honeyman and Norman were engrossed in each other. Norman was asking Honeyman about Fitzgerald, and Honeyman was telling beautiful stories about Fitzgerald. "I never knew you knew Fitzgerald," Minn said, and they went on without looking at her.

They left politely at five, good children, turning down the offer of a chauffeur in favour of a walk. Honeyman wrote them a cheque and made them promise to buy a *batterie de cuisine* at the store behind the Opera in Paris, which they did.

She seldom thought of him now, except perhaps when she snatched the *bain-marie* away from them in the sand-box. But she carried him always inside her like a stone, like a calcified embryo. And wondered if any power on earth could have made her into a Guinèvre when he failed to.

So tonight we celebrate the public Honeyman, she thought. The man who disclaimed artistry at the Cinémathèque, and year after year, with the greatest respect for technique and for form, turned out the best-made crap of the period.

And thought, too, of herself pasted on a peeling Italian wall, all but unrecognizable, a banner labeled *OGGI* over her cleavage.

And which of the horse-operas would they be showing tonight, and which of the Italian comic-books and the French piracies of history?

He wasn't one of the famous expatriate ten. He went to Europe because his third wife was Italian and thought she wanted to go home. She went back to America and he stayed. He found the life good and the work amusing. He made enough to lend money to Losey when things were bad for him. And I stood bored and diffident behind

17

Honeyman, staring at Losey, before I knew there was a Losey, wishing he'd move off and we could get on with wherever, whatever . . . and afterwards he said I was a stupid damn broad and I wanted to hit him.

He and Norman getting on like houses on fire . . .

The first Festival was fun: other film-buffs, other expatriates. Reiner finding a French commercial that said "BALZAC Zéro-zéro-zéro-un" like the olden days at the Ursulines. And always the party afterwards at our place.

But the wave is finished. Those of us who don't have kids are in London, Paris, Hollywood. The big blow-up of Honeyman is torn at the corners. Six sets of staples in it were enough. Reiner's a business head, he's been gradually changing social gears.

He would hate the whole thing. He was willing enough to teach technicalities, but he saw the wash of *cognoscenti* arising from the business, and laughed at them. There were better things to be *cognoscenti* about: books, pictures. It was a means to an end for him, for his generation. He wanted good books and wine out of it, not *das Ding an sich*.

Have to put the blow-up up tonight. Staple it. Inside the walls the plaster will slither down like mice. The grin will loom at me, larger than life, nothing about it natural. The sick lurch returning. He liked my big shoulders, and my greed. Would he like my big belly?

Some days they all throw their food at me and Norman comes home and surveys the mess and goes out again to the movies, and I think, somebody liked me, once, long ago. So now I celebrate with the phonies. Maybe somebody good will come. He wouldn't like that it should come to a dreary lady in a dreary house and one tattered blow-up.

Through the bay window: Jane-Regina mincing. Can I bear her now? Should have tried seriously for an abortion, alcoholics both sides of the family and Annie, me over thirty-five and who needs more kids in the world? Mordie on the hind-legs of indignation at the mere suggestion, though, and the thought, what would a back-street abortionist do with a Loop? Decided to hope for the best: *Sheer plod makes plough down sillion/shine* . . .

Sweet Jane-Regina with her curls, all sheathed as usual in kid, forefinger choosing between the defunct bells.

The one that works turns and makes a sound like Cousin Alice clearing her old throat.

3

Minn stared at Jane-Regina, Jane-Regina stared at Minn. The meeting of minds was always difficult. There were icebergs in the seas between them, ideas about class and competition, values, and the matter of Jane-Regina's eyes which were fine and blue and emotional-looking, so that Minn stared at them hard while Jane-Regina talked, hoping that the words would go away and what made them so emotional would finally be revealed. They reminded her of another beautiful, emotional thing, the sign in the European train windows: *e pericoloso sporgersi*. Which is translated bleakly in Toronto streetcars: KEEP ARM IN.

So she stared into the round China-blue eyes, stared gluttonously, hoping for revelation, and, as the voice (flat, the accents of Edinburgh and Boston imposed on hereditary structure and sinus operations) burled into the evening, remembered the boarding-school prefect, perfect in ringlets, and decided that all that was left of that girl was her flippant way with a skirt, the mark of a former basketball player.

Now she was fingering off her kid gloves. Her shoes and her handbag matched. There is a whole race of women, Minn thought, whose shoes and handbags match, and fell into depression.

19

Jane-Regina was talking about her maid. Once Minn had indicated that she did not enjoy hearing about Jane-Regina's problems with her help, that it was painful to her to be forced weekly to contemplate the difference between a woman who had married a lawyer (and had money in her own right) and a woman who had married a journalist. Jane-Regina said, "Nonsense," and went on.

They really were remarkable eyes. As Minn stared at them, the glittering pupils seemed to enlarge and swallow her up in them. Glycerine, she said to herself firmly, glycerine, and held onto that thought until the story of the maid was done.

Jane-Regina came to people and talked for therapy. She was an active woman and good at everything she did, she had servants and ran her house as if it were an empire, she was through her household tasks every morning by eleven o'clock. She had tried taking courses to fill in the rest of the day, and quenched her desire for self-improvement. She went to meetings, but without conviction. The women's clubs she belonged to were dying dinosaurs. In the summer, she played tennis. In the winter, she visited.

And when she visited, she talked.

There are people who need to talk; there are not enough listeners to go around. Husbands go back to work in the evenings or to the movies, the maids don't understand, the children dash away. Jane-Regina was in love with her husband Oliver, but he defeated sadly her need to talk. He went out, or worse, withdrew. She came to Minn to talk.

"On Saturday afternoons," she said, "we go to Mrs Oliphant's. She lives in a white frame house down near the Heliconian Club. It's a valuable piece of property now — nearly all her neighbours have sold out and their houses are boutiques or townhouses, — but she wouldn't dream of selling. It was her father's house.

"Her husband was a clerk in Oliver's father's office. Her son is an engineer in California. All he ever sends her is dreadful photographs of his children graduating from kindergarten in mortar boards. She ought to sell the house, she's old and dreadfully poor. Very much a lady — she was a McKey — but old and threadbare all the same.

"In her way, she's very resistant to change; and money doesn't interest her. For instance, her pantry looks so unused when we go in to help her with the tea, I wonder if she eats. Whatever it is, I'm sure she shares it with the hippies. They infest the neighbourhood like stray cats, but she seems rather to like them. I've seen her giving them money at the door — and then turn around and complain of the traffic the boutiques bring to the street.

"The house is rather lovely — I can certainly see you in it, Minn, hippies and all. You'd think from the outside that it would be dark and damp, but Mrs Oliphant's fond of pastels and the drawing-room is off-white, and the furniture is slipcovered in faded chintzes. The rug is a hooked imitation Aubusson, terribly grimy — failing sight is a blessing to the elderly isn't it? — white with a wreath of flowers around the edge.

"For her age, she's very active, though sometimes in the spring when she's working hard on her garden there's an edge of exhaustion in her face. She comes to the door in her husband's old buckle galoshes, but she welcomes us nicely and takes our coats and makes us a cup of tea.

"Not many people come calling, or make themselves so easy in her chairs. All her old friends are dead or disabled, so there's only ourselves and the elders of her church.

"Oliver sits down and leafs through her family album. He likes old things. They were handsome people, the McKeys and the Oliphants, though most of them died in the wars. Mrs Oliphant and I discuss the children and the weather, and then we go to the pantry and I help her reach down the tea-set. I don't know how she gets it back up, but I hope she doesn't stand on her rickety wooden stool.

"The tea-set is sweet — Worcester, with spidery indigo blue flowers. And Mrs Oliphant dusts the cups with an honestly grubby tea-towel, while the kettle boils on the high-legged old gas stove. Her kitchen looks like a drawing in an old home-economics book.

21

"I can't honestly say she's a careful housekeeper. I've seen an insect or two scuttle across the pantry floor. But everything's in its place when we come to see her, down to the ginger nuts she keeps in the tea caddy specially for us, which are terribly stale. After Oliver cracked his bridge on one last summer we gave her some Huntley and Palmer's, but she must have handed them out to the hippies, because we never saw them again, not even the tin, which was a particularly decorative one.

"She has a strange relationship with her hippies, she seems to be terribly fond of them, she lets them camp on her lawn and signs petitions for them. It's terribly dangerous, we have to keep a careful eye on her. Some of them are fine, I suppose, you know more about them than I do, but if they're after money for drugs . . . well, she's so old and frail.

"But from time to time odd things appear in her parlour — tin lampshades and peacock feathers and artichokes, leather amulets. I suppose those generations have a lot in common, though as I said her taste is pastel rather than ornate. At any rate, she likes their psychedelic posters and says next year in her garden she'll make them a psychedelic flower bed.

"We've never actually seen her garden, she calls it her 'secret garden'. But in the summer her house is filled with roses and Shasta daisies and sometimes she comes to the door smelly and talking about her compost heap. She can't do anything with the beds out front, there are too many trespassers and cats and dogs.

"So we load the tea-tray with the Worcester and the old brown betty teapot and bring the kettle in to make tea properly by the fire. She leaves her silver service in the dining room. It's black with age now, but she says she doesn't believe in advertising Saran wrap.

"She likes to hear about the office and the law courts. We keep her up to date with the outside world. She won't have television and it's not good for the elderly to live too much inside themselves.

22

"She isn't an open person, but once or twice she has made a small confidence. Once she bent and rustled around in the bottom of the bookcase by the fireplace, behind the basket of kindling, and produced a sheaf of poems she wrote in her twenties. They were about nature and very sweet.

"Precisely at five by the grandfather clock in the stairwell, we all sigh and get up to say good-bye. Oliver loads the tray very carefully and takes it into the pantry. She won't let us help with the dishes, she says she enjoys doing them herself. So we put on our coats and go to the door to say a proper farewell. Mrs. Oliphant always, I must say, looks grateful. Oliver drops a five-dollar bill in the umbrella-stand, which she neither acknowledges nor returns.

"We used to have another old lady in the neighbourhood, but she died.

"Do you miss going to church on Sunday?"

Minn, who was thinking of another Italian sign, the pencilled notice on the paper-towel machine in the Bologna railway station ladies' loo, INSERT A MONEY IN THE ORIFICE AND PRESS DEEPLY THE STUD, swam back through the blue eyes without missing the icebergs. "Goodness no. How would I do it? Have to be up at six, brushing them."

"Well, it's Nanny's day off and I must say I sometimes just send the older two to Sunday School with Oliver. But we always go to Evensong, and the curate and some friends come for supper afterwards — a proper Sunday supper with devilled eggs and cold sliced tongue — and then we go out to the back to Oliver's studio and drink brandy and listen to records while Oliver works on his tapestry. You must come.

"I can't say I *like* Oliver's tapestry: he weaves on a tiny loom and stitches the pieces together, then embroiders them. It's very effective but I don't like the colours he chooses, gold and silver thread over violet and sick green, things like that. Snakelike. His designs are abstract but somehow they come out mediaeval. He's very devoted. He

23

sends me all over town looking for his yarns and threads. I've found the last woman in the world who does decent smocking, so there's some profit in it for me. Still, it's probably good for him, though you'd have thought the age of hobbies was gone.

"It's late, now. You're not looking well; your ankles are swollen; you ought to call your doctor. I wish you were going to the Private Patients' Pavilion, Minnie, you'd have much better food. I've brought you Kate's layette — Nanny had it laundered and put away. It ought to save you getting together another one. If you have to go in suddenly, I can lend you Nanny for a day or two. She wouldn't be thrilled by the neighbourhood, but she's very faithful and good. I ought to warn you she'll run up a fortune in *paté*, she lives on it. You can get it from Eaton's by phone.

"Oliver said he might drop by for your party, even if it isn't yours, really. He's not going to the Honeyman film, it appears there's another new Godard. Are you eating well? Are you sleeping? Are the children behaving? You really must send them off to nursery school. I believe Helene Cohen's very good and she doesn't require an expensive uniform like Tiny Tots."

Minn sat, hypnotised, watching her put on her gloves. She tried to remember who it was at summer camp who could fart at will. "Thank you for coming," she said in a small, obedient voice.

"Lovely to see you. Oh yes, and I've brought you a book, you'll probably hate it, but he's very sensible really. I heard Nanny reading bits of it out over the phone to her friend. She's quite perfect, Nanny, much the best we've ever had. We got her through an agency which gave us an absolute grilling first, and then made us pay her fare and three months' wages in advance. Oliver was livid, but it has been worth our while. She's not too good looking, but she's not old, either, and as far as I can see she has only one fault, she does the most awful things to Melanie's hair . . ."

Minn rose, and summoned her dignity, because after Melanie's hair it was Jasper's teeth. "Do excuse me," she said in a mellifluous dowager duchess's voice, "I have to pee." She sailed out of the room and up the stairs, down the long corridor to the bathroom where she turned on the tap and sat a good long time studying the *Penguin Dictionary of Saints* without seeing the words. One of her moral exercises was not to comment even to herself on Jane-Regina. She let the high flat voice ring until it echoed no longer in her ears, and then eased herself downstairs again.

There in the living room, Jane-Regina was pushing her gloves up her fingers as if that were the most important action in the world, and Poor Richard was standing in the archway to the dining-room gawking at her, looking his most unfortunate self in a miserable goatee that failed to cover his acne, and a tie-dye tee-shirt of indecipherable colour. She hesitated a moment, to see if either would speak, but they did not.

"This is my friend Mrs Magill," she said to Richard.

Jane-Regina looked at Richard gravely. Richard shuffled and mumbled and turned away.

"Did you want anything, Richard?"

"No," he said, and took the opportunity to flee.

"Such a household," Jane-Regina said. "I don't know how you stand it."

This was an opportunity to complain, and Minn knew how to complain. There were whole days when she barrelled around the house muttering against her role of servant to multitudes. Now she looked at Jane-Regina with what she hoped was mildness and resignation and sat on the boxed layette. "Oh dear," she said.

"You must take care of yourself."

"I do, believe me."

"Well, I really have to get home."

Minn said, "Thank you for coming," in a small, obedient voice, and got up to see her out.

Her certain shoes dealt carefully with worn carpet and rickety steps. She looked back at Minn in the doorway. "Do call if you need anything." And went determinedly into the dark.

4

She went back into the living room to watch Jane-Regina get into her car, and thought, God again working in His mysterious way to turn out a new *Believe It Or Not* every day. And was startled, because the voice and the mind of that thought were Norman's. Did he, wherever he was tonight, think Minn thoughts, and alternately rejoice and rebel at the concept of one flesh?

She was glad he had not been there tonight to stiffen at her, fume afterwards about the presence of such women in his house.

Well, she thought, it was good of her to bring the layette. There are the wise virgins and there are the foolish virgins, one knows where she has put me.

But that irritated her as well, as the story always had in church: the unfairness of it, the ones with the full lamps smugly refusing to share. And herself always knowing which side she was on. The righteous with their minds dammed off, their hearts beating evenly, their feet pointed to heaven. Mary-and-Martha, too, something smug and creepy there, ugly morality aimed at women. Some cathedral Honeyman took her to see, with a row of foolish virgins carved in rose-coloured granite: lithe, beautiful mediaeval figures, with goose-throats and smiles like Joan Greenwood's. See, he said, artists always like sinners best.

Where? Somewhere with a lot of lacy carving, signs hanging from brackets. Strasbourg. We stuffed ourselves with paté. Fuck Nanny. Oliver probably does.

She opened the box containing Jane-Regina's baby trousseau. It was exquisitely coffined in uncrumpled tissue paper. The bootees were stuffed with cotton wool. The little nightgowns were of knitted fabric, lisle or stockinette, something English. No ordinary flannelette. White fine

26

embroidery. A purled bonnet. A matinée jacket trimmed with angora. Ribbons of silk.

She looked at it until she found on one of the nightgowns the smallest possible spot, then closed the box with satisfaction. She was good at small-mindedness, she came from a long tradition of nit-picking. She got up and stowed the thing away in the sideboard, on top of the neglected scrabble board, praising in her mind all Chartists and freers of serfs. She had her own bloody layette.

She looked at her watch and wondered how to stay awake until the people came. She never had any trouble sleeping when she shouldn't. She sat down determinedly in the straight armchair at the head of the dining room table, and picked up the book that Jane-Regina had brought.

Shee-it, the new tyranny. *The Challenge of Childhood.* And on the back of the jacket a bearded neo-Patagonian with mild Jesus eyes and a bug's expression: *I know what you do to them.*

But I don't do anything to them, I'm afraid to. That's why I want to wring their necks.

What school does he belong to, then? What's his postulated worried Mum: hand-wringing and hectored? clueless and backward? self-punishing and infirm? overwhelming? compulsive? authoritarian? Is he out to soothe or to advise? Am I a patient, a fellow student or a lady gone very wrong?

Ah — firmness, routine, discipline. You don't run a restaurant. Lead the child calmly and firmly to the toilet and insist that he sit there. Calmly remove the uneaten food and supply no other.

It's an easy one, though. Large-type comment, small-type case-histories, and exercises at the end. If you have mastered this chapter you will be able to master tantrums. Ever tried mastering three tantrums, doctor? Try eating peanut-butter sandwiches.

She snapped the book shut and held her head in her hands. Child-raising manuals continually destroyed her, pushed her against monoliths: the perfect housekeeper, the perfect disciplinarian, the perfect mother. There was no

27

way of raising herself to a decent level of achievement, and no way of accepting failure. The only thing to do was keep away from the literature.

And she kept masochistically returning to it. She read, so she read about what she was involved with. She opened the book again.

Something about it struck her this time, stroked a memory. She had barely read a case-history before her eyes rolled back, she smelled something . . .

First the reek of English alleys in the good English child-books, then . . . .

A damp wicker fernstand.

The war ending. Puberty. The masonry of female mysteries. Annabel MacGregor, best friend Annabel MacGregor the doctor's daughter. The screened and damp, dim side-verandah at MacGregors'. Lying on the floor giggling and wondering at MacGregors' maid's confession magazines. Hunting hopelessly through *Maclean's* and *Saturday Night* and *Chatelaine* and *The National Geographic* and Mrs. MacGregor's *Woman's Journal* that had borders of scotty dogs and a gardening page and funny knitting patterns; searching through *The Star Weekly* and even Alice's *Family Herald and Weekly Star*. Finding it finally, in *The Ladies' Home Journal* : the future cast for them by a feature called "How Young America Lives".

The French term for window-shopping is "licking the window-panes." Minn and Annabel lay nose-pressed to the glossy pages, goon-eyed for the post-war prefab, the (large) planned family, the budget, the payments on the washing machine, the lectures on patience with mother-in-law and husband's self-improvement courses. Envying their grownupness, their pert gir ;ham shirts and everyday Yankee blue-jeans, their *Journal*-designed, home-constructed wardrobes, their willingness to drive jeeps or live in tents or trailers. There was never a mention of inherited silver or neurosis, and nothing in the budgets for liquor or companions for Mongoloid relatives. In the front part of the magazine "Tell Me Doctor" handled sex by writing month after month about menopause and menstrual cramps.

It was their secret world. They had to buy the magazine themselves, month about. American magazines never entered either of their houses. They slept with back numbers and pored over the back section. People not much older than themselves were hatched in the world, managing. And they were all clean, hawk-eyed Americans, before McCarthy and television showed them to be fallible, and Minn and Annabel, sensing their own abnormality, hung each month around the drugstore Punchinello waiting for another chapter of their lives. Normalcy was the most exciting word they had ever heard.

She looked up and around her and laughed at the defeat of that tiny teen-age dream. She herself in this chosen catastrophe, Annabel single still and running her father's practice . . .

Well, she thought, I'm out, and she's doing something. Miracle either of us survived. Walking down the street, hearing whispering voices, "There's Willie's daughter": seeing a finger lifting the slat of a cheap venetian blind.

Wonder what would have happened to Annabel and me if we married at twenty? Divorce? Disaster? She was a fiercer kid than I was. She bit so hard they filed her teeth down. At seven, she decided to be a doctor, and that calmed her. She's more Godwin than Mother now, tight, unforgiving, righteous. There'll be a gentleness in her with a patient that I'll never see. But she's so tough from the struggle with medicine she's inhuman, now. "You'll have to go out and work, Minn," she said last time we met. "Staying home is fattening."

Work? Please, mister, can I dub your newest film? Please mister, can I write your English titles? Please mister, my typing's ropey but Honeyman said I was good at writing the links in a script for him. Fuck it.

Young America got its four kids fledged and rushed into the labour market. If times get worse, they'll have to lay the mothers off. Please mister, can I stay home without going round the bend?

Meanwhile, the children of Young America were thumping up the back stairs again. Their rejection of

29

neatness she did not mind, it was close to her heart; presumably they were drugged to the gills now because someone else had rejected imagination eighteen years ago. What she rejected in them, however, was the fact that however politically oriented and ecologically enthusiastic they were, however open, aware, free, un-hung-up, with-it, genuine and generous to each other, they were pinching her silver piece by piece. It might be worldly and immoral of her to have silver, but what silver she had had been sent over to her in Europe when she married Norman by hard-pressed aunts and cousins who arranged particularly that she should not have to pay duty, and that the pieces should match each other. To let it walk off lightly on bell-bottomed legs was a failure of consideration. She would have to deal with them.

Deal with them. She dropped Jane-Regina's gift book to the floor. Deal with anything. The rent she would pay now for a bee-loud glade. That Marvella's what Mother would call a little snip. And she'd be right.

Christ, what are they shooting into their veins up there? Is it a herd instinct, have they turned into lemmings?

Sell all thou hast and give it to the poor. But it's mine, kids, I'll do the selling.

Who else to rent the attic to? Tried bums, they cut each other up on Old Sailor. Tried Old Sailor, too.

You are not living realistically — last letter from Annabel after her Christmas visit to Toronto. Who lives realistically? Whence comes the gift for realism?

Can't think any more. Ezra told Hadley her brain would melt after she had the baby. Narcissus and I live in disconnected monologue, he beating time from inside me, I maundering.

And Annabel, anyway, what is reality? That dinner party months ago, for someone important because we got a late-and-early sitter, middle-aged and experienced and a dollar-fifty an hour; all I remember is sitting in some citadel of Higher Journalism in Forest Hill where the women all talked about their children. I tried to change the subject for the men's sake, and was cynical about socks. A thirty-five-year-old teeny-bopper in pink lamé and ringlets said, "I can see you don't want your baby."

You are not living realistically. On the contrary, Annabel, I am about to heave myself out of this hard wooden armchair and count my salt-dishes and my spoons. We live as realistically as possible. Because the rent is excessive (so the house is a romantic mistake, find me another) we contract the attic to Marvella. Because babies are cheap but children are not, Norman has to travel. We are living as realistically (face rubbed into debt if the car breaks down) as possible. It is not, of course, realistic for one's body to have conceived yet another child in the 5% margin of failure of the Loop. Put that down to deep-seated destructive urges if you want, or Lawrentian body-think, (Fiona Spaulding saying 'I *know* the exact moment when I conceived, I *know*, I felt it, it was like a little spark') or use your medicine instead of your censoriousness and put it down to mechanics.

Not living realistically? You take care of them all now, don't you, your old father, Gertrude and Alice, and Mrs. Stelmacher and Mrs. Briggs if she's still alive, and all the people in our church, and the teachers and the preachers. I wish I knew them the way you do. You stand by them and care for their bodies and their values.

I do my best, I try. I have some of their grit, maybe only a little, but some. I haven't run away, though I nearly did, once. I was visiting Prue in the Clarke Institute two years ago, when the twins were in arms and Louisa was terrible-two. Prue was sweet and sedated. They were going to let her go back to her children soon, and she was quietly thrilled. I looked around her room. It was spanking new, then, all vinyl, formica and brushed steel and plate-glass window. With not a fingermark in it. From her window in the tenth floor I saw our house near the bottom of the city, and beyond it, the islands. I thought, I could stay here and still watch over them. I could be a sort of absent angel-presence. . . It was very clean and beautiful there.

It was after that I met the psychiatrist at the party who talked about power. Then he said, "She was happy because they had her on happy pills. But she couldn't walk out that front door to her children. You could." And then, "What takes away the pain will take the joy away." Reduced, again.

So all I've got is what reality I know. Western civilization is founded on plumbing and toiletting and may founder on them. I take my kids and I stuff one end and tend the other. It's not a nice job on a bad day, but it keeps your mind off the housework. And it's sexy, if that happens to enter your value-scheme, they're all mouths and underparts, they keep you salivating. After they're a little older, you have to connect the alimentary canals to the sewage canals: that's a hard job, but once it's done it's done. Call me an engineer of alimentary canals, Annabel, and don't get huffy about me and reality. You can go home to a lonely bed after a hard day of it.

So we rent the attic for forty-eight dollars a month to Marvella, a lithe and slimy lady in a tie-dye tee-shirt, braless and nineteen and with no idea of paying the rent by baby-sitting, which was the original idea. Frizz of fixed hair, gold-rimmed children's glasses like Annie's — remember Annie? — and such powers of seduction I fear for Norman's sanity when he is not in Chicoutimi or Katmandu.

It's a nice attic, a Godwin attic. There are three rooms and a sort of box-room with blue and white wallpaper and windowseats. We thought of stuffing it with kids until we saw how steep the stairs were, and the number of roof-slates that are gone, and the way the heat doesn't quite distribute itself. When it's bad in winter they come in and huddle in the kitchen, she and whoever she has with her, her friend Speed, or Eddie the football-player, or that little dark sly girl, Linda, or poor Richard, who is infinitely young and delicate. There are others who've been up there I do not care to know about. They use the back stairs and the back door and the St. Patrick's Public Baths.

Not living realistically? Not running for public office? Not taking shorthand? Not potting? Dr MacGregor, what do you want?

Hope springs eternal for the mother's breast. If she was used up, milky to the point of moo, but wanting to receive rather than give, confused, maudlin, motherless, it was a sign for Richard. He smelled despair and oozed to meet it down the attic stairs. He came regularly to be rejected.

He sat down miserably beside her without speaking. His troubles were in his eyes. He would withhold them almost to spite her.

Never mind, she knew them. "They don't want me," he would say if he spoke.

They all lied, the devils upstairs. Minced down to you and recounted their fantasies, not bothering to contradict yesterday's first. She put her hands on her belly to protect the baby from witless diffidence (Alice at home was fond of eyeing her and saying "Still waters run deep" which was to tell her to stop talking, but in all her travels Minn had never run across a silent man who wasn't witless when he spoke), and let his silence go on. He seemed to want that, and tonight she had the time. He sat and radiated pathos. She was damned if she would say "Om" to him. The evil thought crossed her mind that here was a child who *needed* speed. He wasn't any hippie.

"What is it, Richard?"

"Oh, I dunno."

"Why don't you go back to your aunt Edna?"

"I dunno."

Richard was a push-out rather than a drop-out. When he failed twelfth grade his father called him a snivelling fairy and told him to get out. Richard hitch-hiked to Toronto and landed on the doorstep of his aunt Edna. He had since then had seventeen different jobs and lost his place at aunt Edna's because her boyfriend didn't like him.

Minn could understand that. There had to be something in Richard somewhere, she could even understand his father's calling him a fairy: there was hope in attaching a label to a personage so splendidly null. Alas, he was not even a fairy, he was a slug. Adolescence needed Alice and her broom and Gertrude and her pince-nez to wake it into rebellion.

She winced uneasily when Richard described his mother's letters to Edna on the subject of himself (but at home, Weeping Willie her father himself had taken her over his knee when she was fourteen and opened a letter of his), and the mother-love and the helpless hopelessness were spewed on her, and she saw the blank little suburban house on the thin outskirts of Kincardine, and the earnest Dad, the loving Mum (parents no older than her sister Annie and her brother Alan who died) giving all that they had, and then giving up because that wasn't enough, and there wasn't anything wrong with him and what could they do now?

"What do you want to do with your life, Richard?"

"I dunno." Always the same answer.

"Isn't there anything you like?"

"Oh, sleeping."

"I wish you'd go to a doctor." (But Mordie would burn him out of the office: even to her he'd said 'There are no beatniks in my practice.')

"Oh, I'm OK I guess."

He'd had a job in a shoestore for a couple of months until his hair got too long. He wasn't hip enough to work in the boutiques.

"How's Marvella getting along collecting the rent?"

He looked at her with a little more sharpness than she had recently seen. He was not going to rat: Marvella was his protector. "Oh, OK, I guess."

I won't, she thought, let them do any more tie-dyeing in the kitchen until they pay the rent. And then remembered that she had bought the dyes, because she wanted them to do her sheets. She had watched them doing the tee-shirts and thought, sleazy, no craftsmanship, didn't even boil. And then on impulse given them a grey fitted bottom sheet, which they turned into the sunset she slept on. *Don't trust anybody under thirty* was graven on her heart, because they had turned her old, they and the children; but at times you could make use of them.

34

"Why don't you go home?" she asked.

He was pale and unformed; he turned paler and his features for a moment melted. All the girls Marvella brought to the house had vitality, a knowingness, a beauty under their young uncertainty. Too many of the boys were like this, with something in them squelched. It frightened her. Was it the adored mothers who had let them down, or the undermining fathers? These were the kids born just after the war, the kids out of the *Ladies' Home Journal* and *McCall's* and Togetherness. Four babies in series, budgets, and the resurgence of breast-feeding. It should have worked better than this. The boys were zonked, dead. I want to take them away, she thought, and wondered if it would be better for Ben or worse if the kid inside her belly were a boy. Louisa and Til were fine, but Ben had difficulties already. His male pride was more delicate, it was continually fractured by her efforts to keep order, and after a bad day he went to bed howling and slept with his hands in his pants.

Richard's vocabulary consisted of slang and the few straight adjectives he considered to be male. His home life was great. His mother cooked and cleaned, and after work his father took them all out in the motor boat. He wasn't any good at motors, though his brothers were, or Latin, though his brothers weren't either. He didn't mind water-skiing if the lake was calm. His mother made good bread. No he didn't like reading. Television was OK. He just liked to tool around, you know, look in the store windows and the like.

She took him into the kitchen and warmed him up some stew. Her kids did nothing but paste it on the walls, but he ate, God, how he ate. And it was good to see him eat, because that body would have to fill out and bend one day to the world's work, or even to the rigours of running from it. Kids are so thin, now, she thought. They fattened me up with cream and I rue it, but I learned to eat.

"People coming tonight," she said tentatively.

"Yeah?"

"About eleven."

"Who?"

"Oh, just some people. You can tell Marvella and Speed to come down if they want to behave themselves." Usually they did not, but she had a feeling that the days of celebrating Honeyman were over, that it would be a dead party, that the kids might help.

"Speed's not up there. He's in the hospital."

"There's somebody there who looks like him."

"Gary. And Randy somebody." He washed down the stew with sixteen ounces of milk.

"Did you ever go to Sunday School, Richard?"

"Oh, yeah, when I was a little kid."

"Did any of it sink in?"

"You mean, 'Jesus wants me for a sunbeam' and all that?"

"I was thinking of the prodigal son."

"Yeah, I remember that. He spent all his money and then he went home. They don't want me at home. It upsets the younger ones, they say."

"You should go back to school."

"I can't afford to."

Cripes, he didn't even have the gift of the gab. What did he have, what had he had? What had he seen or suffered? Inarticulate, denatured: what was he like with his peers, who seemed to treat him like a lame follower? She wanted to hit him, slash at him: seventeen years old and dead inside and counting the cost. Why? What do you want most, she had asked so many times, and the answer was always a kind of electric guitar called a Fender that was six hundred or eight hundred dollars new, and he wasn't musical.

It appears that however you live your life it is some mysterious kind of hell, she thought. At his age I was at home and hating it, Gertrude called me Minn and Willie called me Betty and Alice called me darling but she smelled. The maid quit and I had to take Annie for her walks. I had to push a thirty-year-old moron in a bath-chair down the street. It was pain to be alive. And then I discovered that Annie, who was stuck at the age of four,

36

noticed more in her funny way than I'd dreamed of. And I could leave her down in the children's department of the library thumbing *Johnny Crow's Garden* while I went upstairs and flirted with Mother's prize new librarian from England. Taught me "Knees up, Mother Brown", he did. And then the children's librarian would come looking cautiously annoyed because Mother Gertrude was chairman of the Library Board and she oughtn't to say anything, and ask me to take Annie home. It hurt to be alive, but I was alive.

He could read thoughts, Richard. "Tell me what it was like when you went home," he said. She had forgotten she'd told them before she went home that she might stay several days, that they ought not to have a party.

"Oh," she said, at first diffident, "I went home and she bit me and I came back as usual." And then, realising that she was being Richard, and she had to show him there was another way to be, she opened up and swore at one of the old women, and laughed at the other, and told about how she hit her head on the flower pot and said a dirty word, and how she wanted to stay but was not invited, and realised they were too old, and deathly tired, as she would be when the new baby came. She told him, too, what the streets looked like now shorn of elms, and what they had looked like before, and how it was ugly, but it had once been the only place in the world and all hers, and then she had found that that was hollow: and now she thought it was a fine place to have started her life.

"My father," she said, "wasn't a nice man. I've spent a lot of time trying to find out whether Mother ruined him or he ruined her. They were both tough people and things didn't turn out for them. Their first child was a Mongolian idiot, their second died, their third was me. They were both in politics. They must have been as talented as they were powerful. I hated them. They could crush me with a look. He drank, and I blamed it on her. I think now it was probably a case of gingham dog and calico cat." But he did not understand the reference, he had been raised on the wrong reader.

He was most interested in Annabel. "But didn't you even go to see your friend?" And she, listening, remembered being seventeen as well and sitting in Lucy Younger's kitchen, because Lucy was said to be a loose woman, and had been out in the world, had lived in New York and was even rumoured to be Willie's mistress. She was forbidden to go there, but she went. She had to hear from Lucy about the world. And from Morgan at the newspaper who taught her to write, and later to drink. And from the librarian, who liked the knees of Mother Brown. She had sat like Richard with them, asking them questions about themselves.

"No," she said. "No, I didn't. I was afraid to, this time. We were good friends when we were kids, very close. But she's busy and irritable now. You can't talk to her properly. You get so far into a story and she prescribes for you. And she won't talk about herself and she can't talk about her patients. There's no communication."

"You should have gone to her for your doctor."

Too quickly she said, "Oh, I couldn't do that." Then wondered at herself, was it Annabel's special lectures that she objected to, or Annabel's female touch? What she loved about Mordie was his flattery, the affectionate banter that was shamelessly part of his bedside manner. The way, when things were serious, he took on a God-the-Father personality that she would not be able to tolerate in Annabel.

Then she said to Richard, "You're right. I ought to try Annabel. Though I wonder if she'd be sympathetic. Some women get high on pregnancy, they feel better than ever, they love it. I don't. I get fat and draggy and discouraged. She'd be sharp with me for that, I wouldn't like it. It wouldn't help. When you're low, when the stairs get longer and the children get heavier, when they want you to bend and pick them up and you can't, you think you'll never bend again, the only thing that helps is the crassest form of flattery. You can't wheedle that out of a woman who's slogged her way through medical school and buried two fiancés and been a missionary in the Arctic, and then gone home . . ."

38

But he had fallen some time ago, dormouse, asleep against the teapot.

She unfolded herself from the chair and cleared the table. You can't say a house with two dining-rooms isn't big, she thought. This one, an anomalous room connecting the kitchen with the front of the house and containing the back stairs, was dark and gritty. Its one window looked out on the next-door wall. Its floor was uneven and covered with patched dirt-coloured linoleum. Her landlady had offered to replace it with white-and-gilt tile, but she had said thank you, no. She'd have let the hippies off a good slice of their rent for doing the floors, but they preferred more mysterious sources of income. She hoped that Katmandu was filthy so that Norman would be cheered by the contrast on his return.

Reiner had come this afternoon with two cases of booze and some beer and wooden coffins of glasses. She wiped the table around Richard and began to set it up as a bar. Somewhere in one of the higher cupboards they had a brass and mahogany ice bucket. That would make the place more cheerful. She'd get Richard to get it down when he woke up. Washing high cupboards from the tops of ladders was said to be good for bringing on babies, but it was not a resort she cared for.

She wondered wryly what Honeyman would have thought of Reiner, who divided the year into months and the months into Festivals of movie directors. She had never asked him his opinion of anyone below the rank of distributor.

She pulled the liquor out of the box and wondered how Reiner paid for it. He rented an old downtown movie house which was so small you expected to see magic lantern slides from its hairbrush upholstery. Sometimes when she could get Doris in from over the road she slipped out to it, and joined a throng of three or six or thirty to witness another cinematic resurrection. Now that there were so many film societies and smart little coffee-house cinemas (they say the movies are dying, Honeyman, she thought, but they sell more tickets than ever before) he must be feeling the competition. On the whole she preferred to trudge up to College Street to the Cinéma-lumière, but when she could she supported Reiner: he was a friend of Norman's, and what he did had a sort of theatrical *panache*. Last weekend she had pushed and tugged the kids by his theatre for a walk, to see the brave words HONEYMAN FESTIVAL on the scruffy marquee. They had just taken Samuel Fuller down; Honeyman would be succeeded by Abel Gance.

She moved in and out and around the sleeping form of Richard, licking at the room and the kitchen with the J-cloth, wiping and stacking ashtrays, setting the glasses out, rearranging them, wishing she had some flowers.

She wiped the kitchen counters again, and the front of the stove, and the sticky edges of the drawers. She moved comfortably in the big room, and thought of home, because the house at home, though less aged, was of the same era; and thought, too, how odd it was that tonight when she might legitimately have taken herself upstairs with a bottle of Scotch to gruel over memories of Honeyman until his festival began, the sound-and-light show of her subconscious sent flickering across her vacant mind the images of Godwin as if it were the only frame of reference she had ever known. She thought she had made her reckoning with the place years ago, but here in her vulnerable hour it rose before her again, more real and larger than ever before, like a movie . . .

You could, though, you know: and she began to see it in frames. And then hesitated. With some discipline she could force herself to think of the larger world, the issues she ought to be active about: government, ecology, provincial silliness (she was given to writing letters in the dead of night), even her own character, which seemed to be getting out of hand. But that would . . . The state of the world is not an appropriate subject for meditation on dark nights. It leads to the picture of a woman and her children fleeing the holocaust and they are not quick enough and she is not strong enough, and which one should she save?

So what to do? What even to think about, except that place, showing it as she'd dreamed once, to Honeyman? And why not send the mind to dwell on it before it is entirely gone? What else is there to do but watch and pray? Honeyman. All your meticulous work and the machinery of that enormous industry geared to silly stories about never-never-land. Realism was for Russians. The country reaps that harvest now.

But what can you do with a place like Godwin, on, for instance, a Thursday evening, a Thursday in Lent, the night of their prayer meeting? How can you see it and make visible what you see and make it meaningful?

You could shoot it with a very unkind eye. The new chapel will not have mellowed. Its painted concrete block and bathroom glass and paint-rubbed new oak pews will never mellow. The gunmetal war-memorial plaque is the only decoration, besides the flag. And Miss Nix in her purple Ruritanian academic choir-gown with a yellow satin dickie will still come early to rehearse her song. On the piano, because though they bought a Hammond organ, neither she nor Annabel nor the organist (who is teaching piano lessons tonight will play it. Some say they spoiled the look of the place by adding the old Sunday School piano. Some say nothing. The faithful are decimated.

Homesick, am I? Everyone's homesick now. If you don't know how to make a new world, you fall back on the glow of the old one.

The old people enter shuffling, singly or in pairs, not many of them. They walk softly and choose their seats modestly in the middle, never too forward and self-important, at their own and the minister's focal length, and sit silently. Then Gertrude and Alice enter, the tall one stooped, dependent on the arm of the smaller, and settle noisily, in front of the others. Reach for their hymnbooks, squint at the numbers the caretaker posted by the pulpit, fumble at the India paper with their gloves. Put their heads in their hands, their elbows on their knees, sit with their eyes squeezed, praying. Alice looks once between her fingers. Her lips move. It is very quiet.

The minister glides in and when he speaks it is in a sepulchral voice that sends a cool shock through the gathering: "Dearly beloved brethren . . ." He is a sallow and quiet man, young and bald, suppressed and severe. He is the kind they always have. It isn't a piss-and-vinegar religious town and fire-eaters never last. Weeping Willie was the only revivalist they tolerated, and that not forever. Shouting's for Frenchmen and Holy Rollers. There are two men and eight women, cast for thin necks and quiet coughs and antique millinery. The young have their own services.

"Dearly beloved brethren . . ." and the vestry door flies open and Annabel rushes to the piano, quickly displacing Miss Nix. Smoothes her skirt, sits, opens the hymn book noisily, strikes a chord, pounds it firmly. Gertrude and Alice grimace affectionately at her, the minister half-smiles, they remark her youth and her hatlessness, the rush of her red-gold hair and the fact that she has left a busy practice to attend to them, march them through "There were ninety and nine" at a clip that will stimulate their circulation. Who was a child among them, once.

But the real movie is in their heads, in their histories, if you could get it out of them, who never like to talk about the past, because too many memories are a sign of bad housekeeping. Gertrude, in pince-nez at her desk in Victoria College in 1909, the first girl in the district to go to the university; or photographed among her classmates, a covey of middy blouses and dishmop heads, sweet serious faces without artificial alteration, all their intentions open in uncamouflaged eyes, lamplight's little concentrated wrinkles already between those eyes, and at night, little wings of gold passe-partout tape between the eyebrows, the permissable vanity . . .

Or Alice: hitching pony to cutter to drive to town for her music lessons. Snow. Evening beginning in long shadows. The boots they wore then, the big frivolous tam, her back that was always crooked stooped under the heavy overcoat. Fingers not fumbling at the harness, glad to get away. Passing through the village called Muttontown in the

42

valley, where there are cedar trees like Italian cypresses and gangs of boys to snowball her as she goes; thinking, one day I will escape to Toronto to the Conservatory. But she does not.

And the summer of the great haying, that they will talk about, young laughter in their voices as they do. The men are away to the war, there is no help but themselves. Alice giggling and reaching up with the fork as best she can, blistering her fingers on the grain of the handle, forking it up to the wagon. And Gertrude getting down to help while the team stands patient, flanks flinching. The first day they wear their long white cotton dresses, they stuff them into men's overalls the second. They wear poked, frilled sunbonnets and petticoats edged with open-work embroidery they have been taught to do with infinite care and infinite damage to the eyes.

Laughing in the haying, playing tennis in what is now the raspberry patch. Gertrude sent to the farm in the summer to be "built up", Alice in town visiting: cousins and friends.

Later, times getting hard for them. Gertrude marrying the new lawyer in town, Willie Williams, beginning to round on him. Having Annie, losing little Alan. Alice left alone on the farm, pinched and thin in the Depression, looking after her grim father. The night he died, hunting till dawn for big George V pennies to close his eyes, and in shock serving breakfast in her kimono to the hired man.

Picturesque, isn't it? But you'd want something bigger and more dramatic to make a film, the big lurching movement to climax or fall. Something that had a recognizable pattern, something clear. The pioneer family at table cutting into the side of beef, hired man at the end glooming at the pretty table. At a Honeyman picnic nobody ever corked the wine.

But they didn't drink wine, and not many of the girls were pretty. They cooked their beef black until it was dry in the middle. When they had a hired man he ate alone in the back kitchen. The pioneer schoolmistress was not there to get laid, the boys ran away from the fields to the war with gay faces. The farmsteads had a quiet about them we value now; otherwise they were undistinguished. Life did not make art.

And now it tries to look and to be like other places, and succeeds, because it is. If I took Jane-Regina up there she'd say dimly the Courthouse Square was cute but it wasn't very good country for antiques. And I think covetously of that big house, and all the room there is there for us, and then I think no, it's bleak, nothing. What there was is gone, the fight's gone out of the people, they've kept their faults and lost their virtues, with the exception perhaps of Annabel. There's no salt to people any more, unless it's there and I don't get a chance to see it.

She had finished her jobs. There was nothing more she could do without straining her stomach or getting down to fundamentals like the floors. She sent the cameraman away and stopped talking to Honeyman.

Richard was waking up. She could see one open eye between his nose and his elbow on the table. Then he closed it again. The lashes were matted. He was breathing with little sizzling noises. She slapped the Kleenex box beside him on the table and said, "I'm going upstairs to pee."

5

Goodness, what a vulgarism. We don't say pee, Minn, we say tinkle. That's what we teach our respectable daughters, remember?

All the words for it, and the one we choose to use is *tinkle*. The earth-mother sits cycladic on the toilet, the great gush of bladder weighted by foetus follows. She tinkles. The inundation of the world from the fearful mother-cunt, the rain of fertility, the brooding of the goddess: that is called tinkle.

Not only do you tinkle, you tinkle from a tinkle.

Hand round the word-sheets, teacher. "Can I go to the warshroom, miss?" One finger up for number one, two fingers up for number two. Your turn now, Minnie, and don't be too long out of the classroom.

Maybe that's why kids leave home now, to learn the dirty words. Not that they have to go far. Louisa made friends with a little boy in the park; we were both delighted. When we got home, I asked her, clever Mum hoping for Opie-rhymes, what did you play? "Show-dickie," she said, and hid her smiling face. And who told her it was disgraceful?

The mind-body split is nothing to the vocabulary split in this country. Grandmother Morse was proceeding crabwise up the stairs and helpful hypocritical Minn asked "Can I get you something, Grandma?" "No dear," she said, "I wish to urinate." There was a generation.

At camp we called the shithouse the Rose Room. The boys who stayed over August for girls' camp as counsellors called it the Kybo. Betty Morris says poo is the great dirty word at Christopher's nursery school. Where does that leave Winnie, stuck on the Vespasienne?

Oh, the words, the words for it all. Gertrude complains of Annabel's Latinisms, she'd rather be full of windy organs. It's decenter to be indefinite. What's the difference between cunt and vagina, does Latin trim off the hair? Aboriginal castration-legends: women with wolves' heads around their openings. Analogous to crowns of thorns? *Woman with Cannibalistic Aspirations Seeks Edible Fearless Male.* Try that in the Personal Column of the *New York Review of Books.* Who was it in England kept a terrible refrigerator, things brown and hairy inside it, you thought when you reached in for a bottle of lager, so this is what men fear . . .

Why Gods are born from virgins' wombs.

The summer at home Annabel and I found *The Golden Lotus* in the Doctor's study, and memorised the skilful Eastern concubine, legs strung between two plum trees, hammock-held, while her lord and master shied the fruit in. What kind of plums, then? Sloe? Bullace? Damson? Pershore Egg? The doctor when he found us poring over it said, 1) Can you do the Latin? and 2) You will find that the rest of pornography is quite unsatisfactory next to that. He was right. We scorned the girls at camp who canoed six miles to Grise's to buy *White Slave, Black Jade* and *Emerald Queen.* But the best parts were in Latin and we never translated *sugo,* which does not appear then to have meant tomato sauce.

Things you remember. Sex, particularly. In that atmosphere only sex and certain poems, one's complicated feelings about Annie, and, perhaps, spring weather vibrated sufficiently to vividly survive. We used to sleep at each other's houses, go giggling into the night. Then one night, tickling each other, I turned her on her back and discovered that if I ran my fingers lightly over her, practising Hanon exercises, I could make her shudder deliciously. Tickling down her summer pyjamas, avoiding the blossoming and embarrassing pubis, while she shuddered and said, "Don't" weakly, finally rushed into the bathroom and cried. I had never felt such power over anyone.

Felt that again with Honeyman, but in reverse. The first time he came to me I wanted him fanatically, but when the moment came, something inside me cried, "No, no." I pushed him off and sent him blue-balled into the night. If I go to that man he will own me absolutely, I thought. I was right.

Fold up those feelings. Be faithful. Never have them again. Fear of being possessed as by a demon won't happen again. Too much has been handed over. This is Norman's, this is Ben's. These are Louisa's and Til's. Flake of cortex and clit to Mordie until the six-week check-up's over . . .

Concubine on delivery table, strapped, helpless: a little touch of Honeyman in the night.

And in the day, crap-scrubbing.

Poor dormouse downstairs, seventeen, still downy. Limp, fuzzy, lifeless. Must be something in him. Raised up to some impossible nicety, now slavering at a new wave of dirty films. Should get him . . . couldn't do the Latin. Funny how literal photographs fail to excite.

46

No fire in the lad, though. How do they knock it out of them? At two, nearly all of them have it, the daredevil flicker, the courage of ignorance, the fresh, unsoiled ego that resists banality. Is it teaching them dirty, dirty, that knocks it out of them? They did that to us, we overcame it. No pricks to kick against? The first hippies were beautiful, a free spin-off of the Beats, but prosperous, hopeful, ranging, political. These ... Marvella's soiled butterflies trailing limp upstairs, dragging their feet, hunting dope money. My God, if they're typical ... mushrooms in the attic.

Wanting to know what life is for.

She got up, and looked hopefully in her pants. No show.

Impatience. *Impatiens.* Something you grow in your garden between the bleeding-heart and the money plant.

Had enough of suspension, want to get on with living. Even the sprint to warm the bottle, the terrible effort to soothe the colicky child. To deal with something live and squirming and visible. To see its wrinkled articulated feet. I'm limp as Richard, cotton batting in the mind. Hate movies with vaseline on the lens. Good thing Honeyman's dead, how he would squirm at them.

There's no action for me, no direction. Everything is confused and flaccid. The child floats in its placenta, covered with meconium like new white cheese, in a world of Latins and specifics. Where are my hard, dry surfaces?

She stood drowsily in front of the washbasin lathering her hands. There was still time to put in before the night-birds came. It was past her bedtime. She looked around the bathroom and thought, as she always did, that she liked tongue-and-groove siding. A cockroach crawled out of the motor of the electric toothbrush and waggled its egg-case at her. She missed it.

There's your hard, dry surface, she thought.

47

6

She sent Richard around the ground floor with a plastic garbage bag to pick things up like a park keeper, and sat and smoked and watched him work. His hair was short but not professionally barbered, Marvella must have cut it with her nail-scissors. It was mole-coloured on his nape. She thought of Norman and how his hair grew in thrusting whorls on his neck and on his shoulders (they were a pair of apes, and the children were already black-downed; in the hospital once a black nurse had flung up her razor and said, "Oh Mrs Burge, you are a child of Esau), how the whorls matched the musculature and there was coiled life in all of him. He was a small man, Norman, long in the torso but abnormally short in the leg, almost dwarf-like. He had had a mean childhood in the Depression. He was saved by his taut roundness of form, by his intensity, by the blue blaze of his eyes.

No more typical of his age and profession than Richard, she thought. Why blame youth on poor Richard? If all hippies are mole-coloured and lifeless, all reporters are tense, dark and coiled to spring; all housewives are pregnant, the whole world is me. Who laid his finger along his nose and said, I dearly love a generalisation? Leslie Fiedler at a public lecture.

Then she sent Richard round again because he had missed so much. How're you ever going to make out in bed if you're as slack as that? Huck. Runaway. Don't trust anybody over thirty indeed.

In my day these things were arranged better/worse? How old was I? Sixteen? His age? Railway station at night, deserted. Worrying about my bicycle in the shrubs. Mr Butler sells me a ticket to Toronto without comment. I do not hear him phone. Scratchy feeling in the stomach, like

48

midnight feasts of water-ice biscuits, and some fear. Alice's niece Velma died and Alice brought home her bits and pieces, old devotional books, a Pauline Johnson that Alice kept for herself, and a trousseau Velma had been busy at in the San: garments called bust-bodices that Velma wore because cancer was caused by brassieres, angel-skin slips with scalloped edging, fortunately too small, handkerchiefs of good linen with tatted edging and monograms, VT, and a dozen pair of smock-blue wide-legged underpants — all for me. I laughed.

Alice was hurt and said nothing; Gertrude gave me the basilisk's eye. I said, "Well why don't you give them to Annie, nobody will laugh at her?" And the fun started, Gertrude winding up with I never, and Alice placating at first then saying, after all they're perfectly good and Velma made them with her own hands, and without realising that Velma was a relative Alice had all to her own, child of her own unfortunate flesh and blood, child, fifty or not, I laugh again, with sixteen's cruel flash. Gertrude is nearly six feet tall and her hair is crimped in a cruel marcelle wave. Over it she wears a hairnet decorated with small coloured beads at the interstices, beads of the sort they give to Indians. She puts on her public-speaking voice. She categorises my evils. I think I am tough, but I am not yet that tough. I am cruel, undutiful, superficial, lazy, wasteful, scornful, rude, impatient, greedy, unloving, and jealous of Annie. I look for help to Alice, but she does not help, she never can, I am not her child. I am a large lollopping rib of Gertrude, never mind Willie, he's away as usual. Sprung from the forehead of Gertrude, and sprung to sour her life.

I am gated for two weeks and if you think I am going to buy you new underwear when Velma's will do perfectly well, Lady Jane . . .

Sometimes I Lady-Jane Louisa, and she squirms, and, cruelly, I love it. Humiliation by title and tone of voice.

I did not, of course, know that it was legal to run away at sixteen. When, therefore, at dawn the Chicago train pulled into Toronto and I was met by two large policemen, (one took the suitcase, the other an arm) and I was given a cup of coffee in a brown office, and Weeping Willie writhed down at eight whooping with hangover, and slammed me into the Cadillac (why go to the movies when there are so many films in your head?) and drove 200 miles without speaking to let me out in front of the house in Godwin, and drove back to Toronto without stopping — how should I know enough to protest?

And these kids just ran away. No one came after them.

"Look," she said to Richard, "you can put the bag out by the back door now, and see if you can help me decorate the house." She rummaged in the mysterious drawer of the buffet for the collection of paper garlands and folding bells she had salvaged when they were breaking up her aunt Muriel's house. Norman usually hung them up for the Festival. She climbed on a chair and got down the blow-up of Honeyman that Reiner had got them from his distributor, and went into the kitchen to hunt for the staple gun. It was very quiet upstairs. "Where are Marvella and her friends?"

"Out panhandling."

"I hope they don't get arrested."

"They won't. They usually have something to sell, *Harbinger* or something. Marvella makes a lot of paper flowers."

"You tell them for me in case they forget, I don't want any cops here."

"Oh, they wouldn't find anything if they came, there's so many holes in the plaster anyway."

She could see horsemen with crowbars cantering up the stairs and over the children, huzzah hussars, horsebuns on the steps and herself sabre-sliced, beaten. "I don't like cops," she said.

"Why?" He had the ladder and a roll of scotch tape and was ineffectually attempting to affix gaiety to the ceiling.

"Oh, my father drank after he lost his last election and they used to take him in. They weren't very nice to him. It's a sordid story."

"Well, tell it."

She wondered if she should. She brushed it off. "Oh, some people said they beat him with wet towels. Some people said they didn't. There was no figuring out what they did."

"What did your mother do?"

"She was on the Police Commission. She wouldn't believe they did anything to him. She thought he ought to be locked up."

"What happened?"

"He wouldn't talk to me, he wouldn't talk to her. He moved into his office and when they wouldn't let him live there, he went to live with a friend." Lucy. It must have hit Mother hard. "Then they had to put him in an institution, and he died."

"It sounds like a crazy life."

"Oh, I dunno, Richard. They were all trying to do what they thought was right."

She was away at university by the time that house of cards fell down. And working at Elgin House in the summers. She hadn't paid much attention to it. Morgan-the-Paper once tried to convince her that only she could save her father. She went home and tried to talk to Gertrude and ran into such a stone wall that she ran away again. When she thought back, it always seared her. Maybe Morgan was right, if she worked at her mother she could have made things better for her father. But there seemed at the time to be forces involved that were none of her business. Willie openly sneered at her when she suggested she could help him. Alice gave her a look she knew, "If you value your life, don't," . . . And they were having trouble with Annie. Minn shrugged her shoulders and went back to her books and her trays, hoping it wasn't her father who sobbed in the stationhouse every night, and hating herself. She had no courage for flaming swords.

"Are you coming to the party?" she asked Richard.

"What's it about?"

"Old movies."

He almost cringed. "No, I don't think so."

"Then what are you going to do?"

"Would you mind if I took the TV upstairs?"

"God, no, if you can carry it."

"I'll get Gary and Marv."

He was off as fast as his little limp legs could carry him.

7

— Dream, do you? Worry after? Struggle to interpret? Lazy in your life think, once I was someone, earned gold, squandered time, at no man's mercy and at Everyman's? Hunted, rather, some man's mercy, carrying love like your belly now, a ball of butter before you? Why do you bite the hands that fed?

— My husband Norman is in Katmandu among hairless women, picking amber lemons from the trees.

— Working?

— He is writing the last of the Henty books, *With Syphilis in Katmandu*, and reporting on the activities of the Time-Life Pop-Rock Combo, The Pox of Alexander.

— While in your narrow nun-like cell?

— My husband Norman mourns virginity with devotion; thinking me as they all did more careless than I was, having carried my ball of butter until it was rancid and melting and having soiled with it the best silk suit of the late, great . . .

— Build! Organise! Preserve!

— My mother did. You see her work before you.

— We fear you are a downward trend, influenced by your tenants.

— My marriage manages. An asininity is committed from time to time and I am often less than kind, but, surely, there is anger, but no murder. I am often more successful than I have been led to think I deserve. It is true they do not march in line, my ducks (and if they were Annabel's children they would march in line, but Annabel, thank You, has no children) but neither they nor I have been yet beaten and arrested, and that is something. Norman is still with us, and not out of cowardice. That is again, something. Each day I wake *tabula rasa* except for the blurred smudging of dreams, and deal with events as they arrive. I am faithful to my husband (except for dreams); I feed my children milk, vegetables, fruit and protein and eat the destructive puddings myself. I bear domestic upsets with what vengeful equanimity I possess. In return, my husband loves me extravagantly when he can, absents himself when he cannot, and gives me no reason to join the feminists. If he is not generous with spending money, if he keeps me in a tower I resent with reason (the bugs have moved also into the works of the electric clock, it will be eighty-five dollars to fumigate, the landlady will not, and the car insurance comes up this month) you must remember that I tacitly, although it was a civil marriage, agreed, for richer for poorer. We spent our down payment on five years in Paris, and we cannot live as Young America Lives. Books, booze and other stimulations consume our budget. He knew me when I was profligate, the girl whose allowance was gone on the second of the month; he fears inflation, and wishes neither to give up lunches at the Pretzel Bell ($2) nor to duplicate the poverty of his childhood for his children. Therefore we have no $16 housekeepers or $100 nursery schools. He saves, and though I tear my hair, I find it good. I am, furthermore, valuably connected — by this foetus I so desire to spew — to a kind of reality.

    — What is reality?

    — Plumbing, my Lord. The ruby lips connected to the red lane, the infected bronchii depending on the liver. Lights, tissues, sphinctres (wrong orgasms on wrong nights), veins (to be pulled one by one, shrieking like mandrakes from women's legs and put, white worms, in jars), tubes (to be blown or cut according to the season), uterus (pear-shaped, capable of bearing or being hysterectomised), egg-laying apparatus (cystic or fibrous), stomach (seat of good humour) and if I did not mention lights, the partially ruptured gut. One will not speak of faeces, one is overly encyclopaedic on the subject, one watches them each day (for bells, balls, worms, pellets, pennies, looseness, hardness, hair) until one watches one's own, and attends in pregnancy the heaven of enema, which was hell in childhood on the bathmat, and Gertrude wielding the composition instrument: forget it.

— And?

— And, well, glands, my Lord. Ductful and ductless. One does not know enough about them. It is not, for instance, a cancer behind Ben's white and vulnerable ear, it is a lymph gland. There are also my glands. With age and worry they tighten. I think, for instance, if godforbid but if, and wouldn't it be — awful or wonderful? — if I for instance at my age, stage, point of pregnancy, girth, general hairiness etc. managed to fall in love (because fallen in love with) what would happen would be hypertension and general drying-up: guilt withers, jealousy salivates. Damn braces. If the ulterior vena cavae has its reasons, so does the hypothalamus. You should know the rules.

— What will you name the child?

— A name, sir, or a number. A friend called one Tertia. In the school reader, there were Marmaduke and Tod. Harry, Heretic, Harriet, who cares? I want a boy, but I am better with the girls. Already the sex is chosen. Name is self-indulgence. We can date the Shirleys and the Lindas, the Emmas and the Janes. Charlie's a good name, so is Bill. Matilda was probably a mistake, though it works when you think of Eulenspiegel. Will her friends have this kind of radio-oriented erudition?

— Your discontents, are they divine?

— Nothing, my Lord, of fashionable divinity has been allowed to survive. Belief in progress (mother) left me at an early age. Belief in politics (father) can survive only if I think him misunderstood, which he was not. I refuse to have an Oedipus or an Elektra. The awesome thing, however, is that if you push away Moses and the Ancient Greeks at once, you are left with the Girl Guides. "To do my best to do my duty to God and the King (really????) and help other people every day, especially those-at-home." Will it do? Better than Beatles pewling love-love-love war-is-over-in-my-yellow submarine? Why don't you condescend and give us another theology?

— Pass on, oh daughter of Weeping Willie, and of Gertrude-and-Alice Stein.

In Godwin, the beauty parlours were the Bandbox and Stardust and Rene's Beauty Bar. And Hazel.

Hazel was a fat, stocky woman who worked in the back of her house and did permanents and Marcelles. The spring of puberty (rushing over to tell Annabel she'd Started (and the belly ached and the harness hurt, the buckle turned round and made slits in the crack of her bum and Alice did it up too tight and it sat funny and showed through dresses) and Annabel said, 'I did a month ago', having held out, not having told, and they walked with their legs together and in fear (and in the eighth grade on the first day of the white eyelet dress, it indeed happened, the large red spot: she walked home with her exercise book held over her bum, hoping)) Gertrude rushed her off to Hazel to have her braids cut off, and Hazel clicked her tongue sorrowfully and ripped her scissors through the long black hair and rammed her head backwards into a basin like a urinal; washed it; slopped it with ammonia; rolled it lock by lock on electric cucumbers, attached them to an electric octopus: her parents' puberty-present. She was to be a Lady with stranger's fingers in her hair and a head of Medusa-frizz. The world of sacrifice, masochism and confession magazines was broached.

She had seen no signs that her daughters were masochists. Perhaps when labour pains were a necessary and annually expected execration (how many miscarriages had Gertrude had between her and Alan?) one inflicted gradually, through hairdressers, TeenTown, Lenten Confessions, and Intimate Talks, masochism on one's daughters. She went home and cried over her new hair, and Annie came and comforted her. Annie who was permanently Louisa's age. It was from Idiot Annie that she learned to love.

Now her hair was greying. She would have, soon, to grow it long and plait it round her low-relief head, or wear it in a grizzled club-footed bob with square-cut house-dresses buttoning to rolled lisle stockings and oxfords, bringing back the reverse side of the fashionable forties and Marvella's platform soles. Harsh mouths, and military hats and Weeping Willie on a platform, Minn and Annie (they were crazy to put Annie on a platform but they always did it, they believed in that form of Honesty, though Annie was why they had not moved to Toronto) in organdie that crept up to your knees in accordions in the heat and would not go down again when you stood for the Queen (King) and your slip showed six inches and people unkindly laughed, on platforms, even on floats, the parades marching away to the war, the Royal Highland Light Infantry in kilts and beauty and Weeping Willie with his beautiful speech "Mothers of Canada, I want ta pay tribute to the biggest single factor for good, for strength, and, yes, for victory, in this country: to the people who are making Our War Effort not only possible but also — victorious. We will win, we shall win, we are determined to win, because of Your Efforts, and of your Unselfish and Painful and Heroic — yes, Heroic — sacrifices. Gentlemen, I ask you to salute — the Mothers of Canada."

And themselves on a bandwagon, Annie happy and waggling her awful head and Minn weeping with emotion at the songs — parades still made her cry, Norman took her to parades to see her cry because he thought she was mean to the children — and weeping too because over there in the grandstand Grade Six was singing Flow Gently Sweet Afton in two parts after the Red White and Blue and Britannia The Pride Of The Ocean (fancy Honeyman calling it Columbia the Gem when she sang it in bed) and The White Cliffs of Dover with Nancy Britney the soloist in a long dress. Carry On, Carry On, Carry On, with your red and yellow crepe paper streamers for Central School and your blue and white for Dundas, and the micks of O. L. M. in green and yellow. And with a square of red, white or blue cardboard to raise over your head on Mr. McFadyen's signal and make the Union Jack that was going to Save the World for Democracy if you filled in your Sixteen Steps to Tokyo with war-saving stamps. And Minn Williams shut off from it all, up on the platform between Gertrude and Annie, holding Annie's hand in case she did something awful and reciting fiercely to herself, my name's *Esther* Williams to take the pain away.

"*Anna*-bel oh *Anna*-bel." Summer nights and the peewee's call.

"Shhhhh. Mummy's sleeping."

"I've got to take Annie for a walk, come and help me."

"Oh, push her yourself, I'm reading."

You could tell Annie anything, you could push her along and say the wickedest things to her and she cooed and gooed and said "Nice Minnie. Pretty flower." At least nobody laughed at you. They were all scared of your Mum.

8

Stop! Louisa's savaged. In the basement, there. Through the little windows you can see the washer and the dryer and the mastiff. Louisa! Can't get through, can't get through, big as a bullfrog. The dog, he's . . . Norman take off your goddamn lederhosen and rescue . . .

Bells. The whiff of an ugly dream. Men as trees . . . walking on the ceiling. Bells. Too many bells. The ringing and the clinging of the . . .

Gary and Richard were up on the marble table, teetering and swaying on its frail birds'-eye frame, doing something with a hand-drill to the ceiling. Marvella, handing the television aerial up to them, hissed, "They're coming." The boys pushed the aerial through the hole and leapt off the table; it creaked indignantly. They swept frantically at the plaster-dust with their hands and collected their tools.

"We fixed all your doorbells, Miz Burge."

She was awake, now. She stared at the new hole in the ceiling and at the aerial bisecting the corner of the empty room. She thought, now the cockroaches won't have to climb the bloody stairs.

Bells. "Help me up, Marvella." And Marvella extended to her a fish-cool hand. She stood uncertainly for a moment. Bells again. She rubbed her eyes and went to answer the door.

There was Reiner with a big hopeful party-smile on his face, flanked by a pair of waiters in green jackets, frog-footmen with trays. And over his shoulder . . .

Gruess Gott, Sam Talman. The big loopy face grinning gormlessly at her. "Sam. Sam Talman."

Dry leaves, the greenish autumn gloom of the campus, the worries of a mismanaged world interlined with poetry. "You're the first person here. Come on in to the living room."

Dry lips trying to speak. Once upon a . . . The years at university as an island of inaction. Minnie the Mouse of '54 and Ziggy and Sam and meet you inside the door of the movies, and . . .

He has dark small eyes and rolls them heavenward.

Sam: Through Eden took their solitary . . .

Minn: *Le rôle des aspirateurs est devenu de première importance dans tous les ménages; leur emploi est même indispensable . . .*

Sam: Under foot the violet Crocus and hyacinth, with rich inlay Broidered the ground, more coloured than with stone Of costliest emblem . . .

Minn: *Au point de vue de la dépense, on ne doit faire entrer en ligne de compte que celle de l'achat de l'appareil, car pour la con-*

sommation d'électricité elle peut être évaluée à un huitième de kilowatt...

Sam: ... other creature here Beast, bird, insect or worm, durst enter none Such was their awe of man. In shadier bower More sacred and sequester'd, though but feign'd Pan or Sylvanus never slept...

Minn: *La maison étant vide, la ménagère se met au travail. Elle défait les lits pour les aérer, puis retourne dans la salle à manger, débarasse la vaisselle du petit déjeuner, et nettoie la salle à manger.*

Sam: She as a veil down to the slender waist Her unadornëd golden tresses wore Dishevell'd, but in wanton ringlets waved As the vine curls her tendrils...

Minn: *Lorsqu'elle n'a pas l'habitude de laver la vaisselle le soir, elle fait chauffer l'eau à cet éffet pendant ce premier travail...*

Sam: ... which implied Subjection, but required with gentle sway, And by her yielded, by him best received, Yielded with coy submission, modest pride, And sweet reluctant amorous delay...

Minn: *Il est évident que les femmes doivent avoir le souci de mettre leur chevelure à l'abri de la poussière et des mauvaises odeurs...*

Sam: when God said, 'Let the earth bring forth soul living in her kind, Cattle, and creeping things, and beast of the earth Each in their kind.' The earth obey'd, and straight Opening her fertile womb, teem'd at a birth Innumerous living creatures...

Minn: *Quelques-unes sont capables de se faire de seyantes coiffures à l'aide d'un carré de tissu (lavable, bien entendu)...*

Sam: The grassy clods now calved; now half appear'd The tawny lion, pawing to get

free His hinder parts, then springs, as
broke from bonds, And rampant shakes
his brinded mane; the ounce, The libbard,
and the tiger, as the mole,
Rising . . .

Minn: *Les autres, moins habiles, trouvent dans le*
commerce de charmants bonnets . . .

Sam: The bar's open now, what can I get you
to drink?

Minn: Scotch and water, lots of ice, thanks.

She had seen his eyes roving the room, noticing where
fringe was falling, where Ben was sick on the sofa, where
drinks had marred the mantlepiece. She ought to tell him
when he came back about this room, how if you squinted
through your eyelashes it was very beautiful.

Though there was a shabbiness about him now, too.
The room had filled up with frighteningly smart people and
she felt she and Sam belonged together in it: both sagging
in the middle, out of time for the hard-edged physical
outline, and neither very happy nor very rich. No, it wasn't
a question of happiness. Neither of them was comfortable
here tonight.

He handed her her glass, still wearing the wide, sappy
grin she remembered him from school for. "You know, it's
crazy," he said, "I was just walking down Dundas Street
thinking how will I put in the time till my train goes, and I
saw this poster outside a theatre and there you were, tied
to a tree and still smiling. So I looked at the stills in the
case, and I couldn't see your name, but it couldn't have
been anybody else so I bought my ticket and went in. And
after I've sat through a gruelling two hours of Minn falling
over every rock in Albania or wherever they shot it, I went
out and spoke to the manager and said, 'I know that girl,
do you know what happened to her?' And he said, 'We're
going to have a party at her place, come along.' Chance in
a million, eh?"

As he spoke he looked at her directly and cells of
memory sheered off, six different layers tumbling together,

so that she was in the hotel in Avignon daubing disinfectant between her toes and weeping because every day the dry grass slashed her feet through her sandals; and at Vaucluse in the fields about the fountain falling and cursing while the six Corsicans playing Mafia thugs pursued her again and again over the sharp wicked hummocks of the southern summer; and in Paris vomitting as she read the clever French reviews: M. Honeyman has managed to find the only actress completely lacking in class in France; and here, and with Sam and Ziggy watching *Public Enemy* and *The Set-Up* on a double bill, and with Honeyman shouting "But I never wanted to be an actress!" and . . .

"It is crazy," she said, "and very nice."

"So what's happened to you? When did you come back from Europe? Who're you married to?"

"Norm Burge. He's a reporter. We came back in — oh, about '65."

"Well, did you make a lot of movies or was this the only one? You know, when you took off with Ziggy we all though you'd come back for your last year. And when you didn't show we couldn't believe it. Who the hell was going to make the sound effects in English 416? And Ziggy was pretty quiet, and then finally he said, she's making nude movies with a Swedish outfit in Ibiza."

She was amused to find herself flaring out defensively. "Damn Ziggy! Whenever I wanted to talk to anyone, he said 'I got my scholarship to go to the Tropenmuseeum in Amsterdam. We're going to the Tropenmuseeum in Amsterdam.' So I said to him finally, 'Well, go to the Tropenmuseeum in Amsterdam,' and he did."

"So how'd you get into the movies?"

"I met a man who said, 'Would you like to be in my movies?' that's all."

"How many did you make, anyway?"

"Oh gosh, I can't remember, five or six. I guess it was *Ponte Vecchio* tonight, that was the only big part I had. In the rest I was an extra. I was no good, but it was a job."

"None of them ever played Hamilton."

"They turn up late on Buffalo television. Listen, what happened to you?"

"Oh, I'm teaching up north."

"How many kids have you got?"

"Four. You know, after you left, old Hooper, remember Hooper, the way he danced and pranced through his lectures and his gown flapped and we always thought he was going to soar out of the window, anyway, Hooper used to say in his half-assed imported Oxford accent and the spit flying out across the room, 'Can anyone tell us when we can expect our Miss Williams to return from her foreign tour? On dark days in this building I feel I need Miss Williams.' Then all the guys would whisper 'forty inches, forty inches' and he'd get back to whatever he was yakking about."

She shrank from him, then. She could have drawn herself up and said "I am not accustomed to talking to people who do accents badly." She had not wanted to be remembered for her forty-inch bust.

But he had always been crass, Sam. The summer she and Ziggy went to Europe she had tried to get him to come with them. He added up the impulse against the money he would make in the summer at the steel plant and said no. He said he didn't have the money to fart around in Europe. And he was given to making rude remarks about professors like Hooper.

"I saw Ziggy on television last week," she said.

"Yeah, he's done well, hasn't he? You know, the other thing I remember about you was, you used to go home every weekend just about and fight with your mother. Guys used to say, she's a great kid, but don't let her take you home for the weekend, she has this mother."

"You took me home for coffee once and I met yours." She had looked exactly like Sam in a grizzled wig, and bustled around the house shooting dark looks at Minn.

"Well, she was pretty mad at you for thinking I'd go to Europe. We didn't have your kind of money, you know. What happened to your mother after your father died?"

"She hasn't changed a bit. She's still going."

"Still go home?"

"A couple of times a year. What are you teaching?"

"I'm into Guidance, now. I was head of the history department for a while and then I took a summer course. I was down here for a seminar on the drug scene, for all the good it does. I'm looking around for a job in Toronto, too, but things are pretty tight. Joanie used to be a choreographer and now the kids are in school she's getting tired of crummy little towns. Is your husband here?"

"He's away in the Far East."

"How many kids have you got beside this one?" For a moment she thought he was going to rap his knuckles against her stomach.

"This is the fourth."

"So you're keeping up with us. Hell, it's a big party, isn't it? Big party, big town."

He craned his neck and looked around. He didn't seem to be quite the Sam she had known before. Once nothing less than a king or a prince would impress him. Hooper didn't. She moved away a little, to give him a chance to escape and cruise, but he said, "I've gotta grab my raincoat and catch that train. Jeez, I didn't know anybody lived within walking distance of the Union Station. Can I make it in half an hour?"

"Sure, Sam."

"Well, I'll have lots to think about on the way back, won't I? Good to see you, Minn."

She tried to push her way through the people to go with him to the door, but she was badly placed. He grasped her hand and his felt strangely withered and dry. There was something about his eyes, too. Things had happened to him and he was weary. "Say thanks to the manager for me," he called back to her.

She closed her eyes. Time went by and at the time you were too busy to notice it. Suddenly old boyfriends were middle-aged and putting on brave voices. She thought of badly printed albums with pages of snapshots and Speedball lettering and slogans like "College Daze." Forty-inch busts. Skirts to the ankles, and coming back again. Beanies and Frosh pins. She stamped her foot and said "Shit." She was surrounded, and nobody looked up.

63

"Shit," she said again, and squeezed through to find Reiner.

The frogmen had transformed their bar-room by rearranging the table under the blow-up of Honeyman, and moving the paper bells. They had brought their own ice buckets and stacks of virgin tea towels. They had laid out slices of lime on a teak cutting-board and polished the glasses until they glittered. Reiner was leaning against the table talking and laughing and waving his hands. It was his party.

They had met him when he was a waiter in a cheap Czech café off College Street and they were dining out. He had fluttered around them and hesitated and finally asked "Pardon me, sir, is not your wife the actress Elizabeth Borden?" He and Norman took to each other, Reiner's restaurant became one of Norman's night-stops, they talked encyclopaedically of films, and when Reiner opened his cinema he opened it with the first Honeyman Festival, and they gave the party . . .

He was intense and rather beautiful now, successful and glowing. He was no longer the immigrant servant, his diffident shuffle was gone. He turned to her, "Did you find your friend?"

"Yes. It was nice to see him. He's gone to catch his train."

"Good. You've made the house nice."

"I did what I could. Where did you get all the people?"

"Lots of them, aren't there? They're from my new health club. Are any of your friends coming?"

"Betty's Christopher's sick and the Thorntons couldn't get a sitter. Ollie Magill, probably."

"Fine. Oh, I've invited Cal."

"Cal who?"

"Cal Honeyman. He's starting an engagement at the Riverboat for the weekend. I called him in Buffalo. He'll come if he can."

"I thought he'd be in jail."

"Minn, you are so prejudiced. Try to be a good girl if he comes."

64

She was not sure she felt strong enough to see Cal. "Maybe I'll go to bed. I could use some sleep."

"Go and look at the people. They're pretty tonight. I'll get you another drink. Scotch, isn't it? When does Norman come back?"

"Bloody well soon, I hope."

He handed her a drink and frowned at her. "It's OK, Reiner, I'll be a good girl," she said. Knowing her bed was covered with coats. She went into the front room.

The people were a new breed, smooth, hairless, beautiful, the women all bones, in chains and belts and great greased hoops of hair, wearing elastic cat-suits or Manchester-print dashikis, coloured wooden baubles hanging from tubular arms. They shimmered and glittered and turned with canned animation towards each other, eyes rimmed like daisies, mouths pale, strong white teeth and massaged gums flashing. Small breasts tittered under silk and elastic long arms reached for cigarettes, thin elbows bent. Pale men wore black pullovers and sex-symbols on gilt chains around their necks. Two fair Christ-bearded ones revelled in African dress. The women were tanned, no faint white Saxon ghosts waiting for sunshine.

More came: men and women in fluid tunics of crushed velvet, patterned silk, colours shimmering. Again, feral amulets, again, great wafts of hair. Women oiled and limber as black women. They moved in one force to the bar, and pushed back again to the front room, fluttering their hands and raising arms to hair-dos. Their hips were slender, their pelvises stood out dangerously. They seemed a different race.

"Cigarette?" A man with an Australian accent.

"Thanks."

"It's bloody hot. You'd think they'd open a window. Light?"

"Thanks."

"I didn't think much of the flick, did you?"

"Dated and boring."

"So right."

"Ta, luv."

In my day, she thought, Australians wore fishermen's knit pullovers and lived exclusively in pubs around Earl's Court.

It was no longer her day. She could read no expression on the faces which surrounded her. There was uniform jubilation as they waved their glasses at each other, but they had no age and no station. She hunched in the corner staring at them, wondering if they had sprung from the foreheads of land developers to fill their white apartment towers. Then she saw two men rapping the plaster with their knuckles and looking for the beams in the ceiling, and was comforted. Human nature had not changed.

"Irene!"

"Gail!"

"I knew you'd come. How's Penny?" The two heads surged together in the crowd, shutting out her view. They were small and featureless and primed to gossip, they reminded her of distant figures in vaginal deodorant commercials. "And now, from the people who brought you BO . . . " she said, knowing no one would hear her.

People from everywhere. Getting a bad ear for accents now, too long away from Europe, but . . . there's Catford, good God, and there's the Midlands. South Africa. Flat Ontario, getting flatter as you go west. American nasals of the border towns. Even Westmount, almost succeeding in being both Mayfair and Washington Square. Slick people. Hopeful people. Some one of this gang has stood on the top of the Toronto-Dominion Centre and yelled to the islands, "A nous deux, Toronto!"

The thought sickened her. Last week in Godwin a face had made linger past her green light, a face so gnarled (though young), bony and ugly, animal, strong, overwhelmed by nature, that she sat and stared at it until cars honked behind her. It was not a happy face, it was white, set, and tense. The bone structure of a boxer set, with a bad complexion, on the body of a young girl. She watched it cross the road and held up traffic while she looked at it. She expected to see its eyebrows growing out at her, it was so alive and painful in its animality. There was no face like that here.

A man was wedged against her by the crowd. He backed away from her belly, giggled, sent someone's drink flying behind him. "Isn't it a marvellous house? " he asked. "Fourteen foot ceilings."

"But could you live in it? " she asked.

"I went upstairs," he said. "There seem to be babies all over the place, but there's the most wonderful curve in the hall. I don't suppose it *does* anything, there's no structural reason for it, I fancy it's hollow. Imagine that nowadays. Nobody builds like this any more."

She rapped the wall behind her and heard the sound of loose plaster scuttling down.

"You're right," he said, "forty thousand at least to do it over. All the woodwork's loose. But I absolutely adore that bay window . . . " he wedged himself away towards it.

Seeing that she, too, was free, she backed out into the corridor. Another gust of people at the front door, and not her job to greet them. Reiner slid by without seeing her, "Coats upstairs," he cried.

She followed them up. "Watch out, the bannister's loose," a woman said.

"Don't panic, Lizzy."

"And don't slide down it either." Huge guffaws. These would be older.

The bathroom was occupied. Her bedroom as well. They had turned on the lights in the front room and were talking among the toys. She went into Louisa's room to see what the noise was doing to her; found her lying on her back, lips muttering, one arm flung out. She looked thin and vulnerable. "Love from the girl with the forty-inch bust," Minn whispered to her as she covered her and folded her arm under the blanket and kissed her.

The twins' room had a gloom of light from the alley and a carpet on the floor. It wasn't uncomfortable, she had slept on the floor between them when they had had winter croup. But before she could settle down she knew she had to attend to them. Capillary action had moved the piss to the armpits of their Dr Dentons. She worked silently, cursing the acrid taste of the diaper pins in her mouth.

67

Change, push, shunt, manoeuvre. Easy when they're pink and passive. Ben's thing sticking up like a pointing finger, what's he dreaming?

Til was sopping too. She mopped their sheets and folded clean receiving blankets over the wet parts of the cribs. Bugger to change fitted sheets in the middle of the night.

The bathroom was busy, still. She left the wet diapers on the changing table, one more thing to feel guilty about in the morning, and, finding a tin toy saucepan for an ashtray, settled herself on the floor against the wall, wondering how she would get up again.

Safe in the warm breath, among the animals. Spring at Uncle Richard's farm, perched on the calves' manger talking to them. Louisa impressed when I showed her how to call a pig at Black Creek. Pigs come when they are called. Their noisy breathing, quicker than mine. Temptation to synchronise.

Times like this they seemed all the world to her, richer and better than anything because they were newer. She was caught up in a fallacy she recognized, she had to think of them this way because it was the only way to make breeding tolerable, but she sat and rested and loved them, and thought about other fallacies.

Godwin was two hundred miles to the west, a town that wore its railway station at its centre like a rhinestone in a belly-dancer's navel. It did not have a good reputation. It was said to be closed, snobbish, and polluted. And nobody interesting had ever come out of it except Willie Williams and the readers of *Flash* and *Hush* knew all about him.

Honeyman liked Godwin stories, up to a point. Norman liked Godwin stories, up to a point. There was nothing else like them except all the other tales of home.

Funny, she and Norman saw *Pollyanna* when they were in France. In English it must have been cloying, but in French, with a dubbed Jimmy Bean calling "Pol-ya-*na*, Pol-ya-*na!*" outside the white frame castle, she wept for home. Which caused Norman to feel grossly disappointed when she took him there.

68

Last week, the rift in the winter weather had pushed her out of the city westwards. She had an obscure fidelity to the place, and a viscid, always unsatisfied desire to feel loved, to be thought good by them. And a need to see fields again.

She packed them all into the car and thought, this is the last long drive I make, before I have the baby. Her belly pushed the horn when she leaned to look in the rear-view mirror, and the safety-belt would not do up. She handed out cookies and buckled their straps, and drove miles out into the flatlands, the marsh country where creeks run oil and farmers burn gas off through chimney-stacks, and the water has to be brought fifty, sixty miles in pipelines and the towns burn because there's not enough water for hydrants.

Her country, road-grids die-straight, the last southern county to be surveyed. Flat, bleak villages composed of poor churches and Brand X gas stations. She knew most of them, Gertrude or Alice had had a relative here, or Willie taken her out campaigning there.

Coming into Godwin, she saw there were houses now, down in the creekbed beside the willows, which were green and yellow. New ranch houses, with woodwork in coral and cream.

The children were asleep. Gertrude and Alice did not know she was coming, she did not go straight home. Because she dreamed they were dying, in trouble, they were not dying or in trouble. They might not want to see her. She had time to look around.

Down Main Street, past the Anglican Church and the pillared Carnegie library and the repainted railway station, its grey and vermilion gaudiness and newly designed chic lettering at odds with its gingerbread. She went past the cigar store where the great wooden Mr Punch had stood, the first thing she loved in the town at all (she remembered putting her face against his great enamelled rotundity, and shoving Annie off him), which she had last seen priced at $3000 in an antique shop in Toronto. She went past the Hat Shoppe and the Bandbox Beauty Salon and the other western storefronts updated with cracked tile, to the square her great-grandfather Morse built with his American patent cement block machine: the park and the bandstand, the post office, Central School and the Morse building, all equally squalid and squamous and indestructible (for Morse's patent cement blocks do not burn), all meanly designed and meanly executed, the work of her own ancestors. She turned sarcastically to sleeping Ben and said, "The blood that built that runs, diluted by several alcoholics', in your veins," and parked the car to drink the buildings in.

The old man must have designed them himself. She had seen his portrait, he had a long face and dark squinting eyes and a narrow forehead, and they were like him, dour and tight-fisted. Wherever an arch could be crippled in its clumsy effort to soar, wherever a window could be darkened or a keystone disproportionately narrowed, it was. The compound had all the atmosphere and none of the idealism of Victorian slum housing. Norman whooped and hollered whenever he saw it, called it "Old Morse's Grand Design", and she coveted his detachment and could only console herself for their ugliness by thinking that if the buildings had been good — light Georgian brickwork, for instance — they would now be gone. Anything delicate the weather would decay. These — it would take a squad of Weathermen to dent them. And they didn't even bring in any money any more.

On the bench in front of the courthouse, a new generation of old men sat watching and spitting. She had hated passing them on the way from school to the post office. "Willie's daughter . . . Willie's daughter . . ." She thought of getting out and going inside in the hope that she had mis-remembered the interior, that it was in reality colonial and charming and *folklorique* like the courthouses at Niagara-on-the-Lake and Cobourg, but she remembered the reality too well: thick sticky paint and general architectural heaviness. It would take another hundred years for that to thrill a human heart.

She drove past the Morse building (tenements and Willie's office and the thrice-burnt Maple Leaf Cafe) down streets named for generals and peninsular battles, generals, governors-general, reformers, wives of settlers, trees. She began to feel the tide of home. What will I tell them? I haven't mentioned the baby. What will they say?

They never invited her home. They expected her to turn up periodically, and she did. She supposed that they complained to Annabel that she didn't care a tap about them, but if she tried to fuss, to arrange visits ahead of time, to invite them to Toronto, they grew stubborn. They wanted, she thought, to be left alone until they were lonesome, and then to conjure her out of their prayers. Alice sometimes hinted in her letters that she neglected them, but could be forced to renege on her complaint by the suggestion of a winter visit: they had a justified horror of the damages of a juvenile indoor invasion. So, she supposed, they would now be more or less expecting her. When the good weather came, it was time for Minn.

The first married visits had been ghastly, each side expecting praise and receiving blame, Minn and Norman blenching and wincing with their new European sensibility, Gertrude's jaw locked in constant disapproval. But age had mellowed the old women, and the children had loosened Minn's emotions. There were things she had become able to understand about her mother.

If she stayed longer than a day she still came back in little pieces, and Norman would ask her why she did it to herself; she could not answer him logically, there was the one factor of having your children's reality verified by your mother's acknowledgement, in her own case a kind of negative blessing in the failure to lay on hands, and another factor, that of her own spiritual weather, which required cyclical returns to the countryside. "It's a thing I do," she would say to him.

They were standing out in front of the house now, Gertrude and Alice, a pair, a division of labour, a psychic split. Her mother the large one, commanding in port-wine crepe with corset-knots protruding; standing on the verandah, pointing. Her hair was crimped and thinning and bravely blued. She had cold eyes like puddings even from far off, and a tight, resentful mouth. And a presence, a regal presence. She had commanded battalions. You knew that from the way she stood.

Alice was the little, faithful one on the lawn: black-eyed, hunched, humped, shrunken, horny, and harbouring under her skirts the perennial and ineradicable smell. They were inspecting the nascent flower beds, both cardiganed and stooped, one dry, one flabby.

Their blood runs thin, she thought, but they're alive. The house needs painting.

They were turned towards each other. Gertrude was pointing to one of the shrubs with her umbrella. For a moment they locked into place as though she had driven away twelve months ago and left them tethered in that pose. She held her breath and wondered if it was too late to turn back.

In the dark, Til began to cough. She had a funny deep Jean Arthur voice; she had coughed in it when she was born. Minn levered herself up, all vigilance. The coughing stopped.

Minn opened the door. The noise of the party flooded inside: fat laughter, and names called, shoes clumping on the uncarpeted wooden stairs. It sounded friendlier than before. The bathroom was empty. She took the diapers to the bathroom, washed her hands, looked in the mirror at her raddled, midnight face. She could try to sleep on the twins' floor, she could go downstairs again. She went downstairs.

In the living-room, the crowd seemed to have changed. The boiled-shirt set had replaced the beautiful young people. The women were larger, and the men's only flamboyance was in their cufflinks. Shorter hair and lantern jaws, arms moving indecorously. Big eaters and drinkers, these. Faces all vaguely familiar, but none ... yes, Oliver.

"Hi! So when's the big event?"

"In June, if you can believe it."

"Jane doesn't. She's got Nanny primed to leap in."

"Oh, I wouldn't . . . "

"Oh, let them, let them. When's Norman coming back?"

"I don't know. They keep extending his tour."

"He's sending good stuff in."

"I hear you're weaving."

"After a day at the office I get an itch to do something with my hands." He held them up. They were odd hands, long fingered, but bulbous at the fingertips. She wished she knew the sense from the nonsense about hands. People were always saying artistic hands, musical hands. What did they mean by it?

"Can you read hands?"

"I'm behind, I haven't even got onto astrology yet. Who're all the people?"

"If I'm staring at you soulfully it's because you're the only one I know."

"Oh well, new worlds to conquer." He was beginning to try to extract himself from her company. He was very polite, but uncomfortable. A little man with big glasses, nervous, darting. Stupid to ask him about his tapestries, he'd know Jane had been talking, he'd be embarrassed. She thought of sending him to get her a drink, thought, I don't need another one, wondered what to say next, and was rescued by a large man who gripped Oliver's shoulder and said, "Attaboy, Ollie, tell me about the lien." He excused himself.

She found herself staring at the back of a pair of arms much marred by cellulite. A worried face turned towards her, a wide mouth opened and said, "Do you love your husband?"

"What? Me? Of course I do."

A big woman, very tall. Forty-five, fifty. Patroness type. A little shaggy for the Art Gallery Committee. Maybe on the edge of the Museum. Money somewhere. Good family. But something that does not . . .

"We don't usually come to these things, but Bill was longing to see Avignon again in this — *Ponte Vecchio*, is it? I can't say I thought much of the story. did you? It all seemed so pointless, chasing that one young girl around. And then they invited us here. I like the house but I can't say I envy the poor woman who lives here. We used to live downtown but it's all so difficult. The whole of one's life in Toronto is organised for living farther north, don't you think? Of course the Beaches are coming up again, but ... You know I was just accosted by some little snip of a girl who's going around and saying to people, 'Do you love your husband?' and slipping away again. I didn't mean to imitate, but now I'm a little upset. I couldn't think what on earth to reply. I haven't thought of anything so complex for years. When things get difficult I go out into the garden and rip up nightshade, it's parasitic and poisonous, one has a spurious feeling of usefulness. But love! Did I love my husband! Well, I said, what's that got to do with anything? But she was gone, then. Really though, I suppose it was very important, once. I can remember feeling desperate and fainting beside telephones, but now ... at our age it simply isn't relevant, is it? You have to get on with your life."

She wore her hair in a braid knotted on the top of her head. She had watery blue eyes and a figure that was upholstered rather than dressed. "You come to the point," she continued, "when the garden is simply more important. You can't sit thinking, does he love me, do I love him, when the nightshade grows up and twines around the lilacs, and gets into the scarlet runners, can you?"

"I'd like to have scarlet runners," said Minn.

"Well, dear, I'm sure you would." She laid a warm hand on Minn's shoulder. It was odd to be touched. Then a man turned her away, and Minn was disappointed. She would like to have known the woman.

There was no one to talk to. She stood and thought, do I love Norman? Does Norman love me? There was no answer. The woman was right. Love was an idea you lived through and came out on the other side of. It was slowly replaced by the necessities of devotion and duty. But it manifested itself periodically in little misplaced surges of carnality. and went away again. The spirit nourished on

Lorna Doone and *Jane Eyre* and *Le Grand Meaulnes* did not give up adventure easily. She knew as she searched the buzzing crowd for a likeable face that she was looking for a man.

The house smelled, too or again: smoke and damp brought out a century of odours with overtones of plaster and pee. She squeezed out through the hall and bent to pick up a matchbox toy Richard had missed. It was too much effort. She shoved it with her toe into the crack beside the register. The register fell down. Class is maintenance, she thought as she hunkered to fix the register in place. There was a fur of soot around its edges. She had replaced it a million times and never thought to wash it.

In the relative quiet of the hall she could hear Oliver Magill's voice, slow, measured, with the hopeful ironic humour of the shy man in it. He was saying something about texture on film. Maybe this time he would talk to her. She went to join him.

But he was talking to Marvella, who was wearing an old woman's grey lace dress like a silver cobweb, and cast-off tap-dancing shoes and a secretive smile. He was showing her the hallmark on the silver sugar bowl. They were about the same height, they looked well together.

She pushed by them smiling and was caught in a group of women at the end of the dining-room table. They were her own age, but tough and professional. They all wore black, tailor-made, figure-concealing dresses. "What do *you* think?" one of them asked her, and stared at her belly.

The second, who had long black hair and yellow eyes like a cat's, said, "They're the first ones to bitch if a male doesn't open a door for them, aren't they?"

"They're all dykes," the third one said.

Responses welled up in Minn like bubbles, but she dismissed each one separately as rude or illogical. She was physically trapped in the group now, and she did not like their style. There was something aggressive about them. They wanted her to choose up sides in a game she did not like, it disgusted her when people wanted to divide the world into two sides and ignore its multifariousness. But she decided to be polite if it killed her.

Then Yellow-Eyes grasped her shoulder and said, "Well?"

"What's wrong with dykes? They keep the population down," Minn said. She wrenched herself away from the woman's hand.

They moved in on her, and stared at her, trying to see if she was serious. She felt that if she said the wrong thing again they would pull her hair. She reached desperately for something peaceable to say, found herself blessing convention, wishing she had not left it so cheerfully behind, that she remembered which of its dictates would fish her out. Norman in this situation would do a bit; she did not have the courage.

"Thank God the winter's over," she said, remembering weather.

"You're not really in favour of Women's Lib," one said accusingly.

"They have a few points," she said tentatively, trying to think of some.

"Such as?"

"We ought to have legal rights over our bodies."

"Not going to achieve that by throwing your bras away, are you?"

"God, I don't know. Anything for a change, I guess." She was pinned and wriggling, now. She didn't belong to the organization.

"Who feeds you? Who buys your clothes?"

"I earn it," she said defensively.

"Could you earn as much if you went out to work?"

"I doubt it."

"Because you couldn't take the responsibility. You want it both ways, the doors opened for you, the bread slung into your mouth, and yourself the boss. You want to be on top. Who's going to look after the children?"

"I figure, you make your bed, you lie in it," snarled the one with the yellow eyes.

Minn caught the eye of one of the waiters and signalled him to bring his tray. "It's such an old quarrel," she sighed, and pushed away from them. But it was not to be so easy. "Do you think it's right," one of them said, "to break down the entire system of division of labour?" She was tall and weedy and wore harlequin glasses. Her bosom was thin. She had drunk a lot. She had skinny arms.

Go away, I don't want to sit down and hack it, Minn thought. There's a seam in myself I don't want to open. I'm busy pretending to be happy. "No system is fair to everybody," she said as blandly as she could. What the hell were they doing at Honeyman's Festival?

"I don't know who you are, sister, but if you haven't got things figured out any better than that, you're in for trouble."

They circled her now like harpies. She wanted to strike at them and get away from them. What did they want her to say? They looked as if they ought to be out burning Dr Spock. They were taking the wrong line for their looks. She was confused.

"Look," said the one with the glasses, who also wore round metal beads, "you're going to have a kid, that means making a lot of decisions. What're you going to bring it up like if it's a girl?"

She held up two fingers and smiled. "To do my best to do my duty to God and the King and . . ."

But they were not put off. "Look, a bunch of dykes down in New York are . . ."

"Lay off, Sheila," said the one with the yellow eyes. "Maybe you're insulting her breed."

Sheila closed her mouth. Minn stood like the cheese in their circle, contrite. "I don't want to argue with you," she said. "I don't want to argue with anyone." Yet something of Gertrude's authority had crept into her voice. Uncannily, it subdued them. They stepped aside and let her go.

The room was clearing. She found a little space to stand and breathe in by the bay window. A lot of the people had gone home. She was left with the dedicated drinkers, the late-comers, the people who never wanted to go home — bed being the beast that waits.

These people look strange; it's unhealthy, she thought, the way we keep our own company too much, we stick with the rowboat international set, it gives us a pleasant feeling that the world's a scruffy club. Oh Norman, Norman, come bloody well home, and bring your funny friends with you to drink cheap booze and talk about their favourite bad hotels. This house is beginning to look like the lobby of the Holiday Inn.

Down at the end of the dining-room, the three harpies had seized another woman's arm. Around her, men were talking business and women were talking babies. Oliver and Marvella were not in sight. Blessedly, the chair beside the sofa was free. She sat down on it and half hid herself behind a fern.

She had seen them before they saw her, and still wondered for a moment whether to run away. The Alice turned and came running, and by the time Minn had blown the horn with her belly getting out of the car and wakened the children, Gertrude, too, was aware of her, and had moved to the top of the verandah steps to receive her.

But first she unstrapped her children from their thirty-six dollars' worth of car seats, and watched Louisa barrel into Alice's apron and move back from the pong, and barrel into her again. Alice said, "Goodness, I'm too old to pick you up," and in one movement sidled to kiss Minn and reached for Ben and Til.

The children looked sweet. They had slept most of the way and were reasonably clean, except for crumbs and a sinister hang to the twins' rubber pants. She made them terra-cotta coloured smocks and embroidered them with black on the yoke. They looked archaic in their Attic colours: solid, mop-headed children planted on the lawn. It was good to do something visual with them when you couldn't do anything else.

She looked back at her mother. She had always looked the same, there was comfort in that. They called me Esther Minetta, she thought, after a street in New York and a queen. She knew what Gertrude was thinking, wondered when she had first learned to absent herself under the gaze of those watery, wilful eyes. "I just came to see how you are," she said. "Sometimes I worry, you know."

Gertrude eyed her belly and said, "Well, I never."

"I thought I'd better tell you in person."

"You can phone after ten for seventy-five cents now and talk ten minutes," said Gertrude, looking pleased all the same. Minn said, "Louisa always says 'When I grow up, you will grow down.' " Gertrude was not impressed. She began slowly to lead the way into the house. She had counted her grandchildren and that was as close as she wanted to come to them.

Minn was about to follow her when she saw Bennie heading for the road. She dashed after him, as usual expecting her belly to jiggle like a paunch and amazed that it did not, and angry that it kept her from quickness. She tried in that instant to think of that and not what the child would do when he saw her coming. Once he had dashed across Bay Street (he was harnessed but his middle name was Houdini) and she had been left screaming on the far side holding Louisa and Til, thinking O God if he's killed at least it'll happen only once, until a firm middle-aged woman marched him back against the traffic and helped her strap him in, pulling the buckles tight while he fought. And she thanked the woman, and cried. The woman looked like a prison guard. She said, "You'll find it helps to hold them by the upper arm," and returned to the other side of the road.

Roads: always the menace, the divine attraction: "Ben!" He did not turn, he continued to jiggle along parallel to the curb. She had almost caught him when Alice cried, "Cookies!" Ben staggered, stopped, and returned.

She was red and hot and out of breath. She went up to the verandah steps to meet her mother. She hit her head on the hanging flower pot. "Shit," she said.

Once in the cool gloom of the house she was powerless, without initiative. The smell of furniture polish sapped her. The hopelessness of reinventing this dying world: piano and parlour and jar-rings sewn to the corners of domestic oriental rugs. She took Ben upstairs to change him, and showed him the rainbows dispensed on the landing by the bits of cut glass in the oriel. He tried to lick them. Upstairs, she laid him on the bathroom linoleum. He was quiet, subdued by having a new ceiling to stare at, and it gave her a pause, a chance to adjust herself, to change her pace. She washed his bottom and told him it would hurt less if he went to the toilet. She ferreted in the medicine cabinet for something to put on his diaper rash, and found a dusty jar of vaseline, a ball of cotton out of a pill-bottle, a thousand old prescriptions, Alice's spare dentures, and a small art-deco tin of powdered nail rouge. He giggled as she rubbed the vaseline on and got up before she had his pants pulled properly up, and was out the bathroom door while she was still rinsing his diaper. She went to the toilet herself and heard him cantering around in Annie's room. Long time since a child's feet had made echoes there. Ben came back and stood uncertainly in the doorway. "What did you see, love?" she asked him. He took her hand and led her into the big nursery. "Annie's room," she told him. They stood for a moment beside Annie's enormous stainless-steel crib, which was still made up. It spooked him. If they stayed the night, she wouldn't get any of the kids to sleep in it. She'd have to drive back to Toronto. "It's all right, Ben," she said.

In the kitchen, Alice was dealing out molasses cookies and cambric tea. Minn took the tea-tray in to her mother.

And sat beside her man's leather arm-chair, listening to her knitting needles clicking. Her hands were knobbled but she went on knitting still. "It's for the Red Cross," Gertrude said. "I didn't know you'd need anything."

"I didn't want to tell you. I thought it would upset you."

"It's hardly necessary to have so many these days."

"Accident."

"You're as big as you were with the twins."

"We're pretty sure there's only one."

"I hope your doctor knows what he's doing."

"He does."

"I suppose you'll want to go over and see Annabel. She's extremely busy."

"No, I came to see you."

"I wonder you don't worry more, knowing about Annie."

"It's not necessarily hereditary."

"Well, I had you when I was forty and you're nearly that yourself."

Which would make her seventy-seven. Minn was obscurely pleased to hear her lying about her age. She was eighty-two if she was a day.

"I certainly hope you're eating well." The needles went on clicking.

A procession of peanut butter sandwiches passed through Minn's head, followed by beer-bottles, celery sticks and the tag-ends of jars of baby food. Followed by the recurring cravings: oysters stewed in honey, wild boar in sour cream, saddle of hare, Charlotte mousse, syllabub and battledore. "Yes." Honeyman had loved her for her greed and taken her here for venison, there for larks on a spit. To Venice for quail on polenta, to Nice for *socca* and lemonade-wine. "Yes," she lied. "We do ourselves well." And thought of the game butchers in the 15th *arrondissement*, the cups below the hanging hares, the dripping deer. "How are you, Mother?"

"Annabel takes my blood pressure once a week. I seem to be fine. I forget things sometimes. I miss Annie."

"So do I."

The needles stopped. "Now, Minn, you know you were jealous of Annie."

Her back was straight still, and she held her head up. She was not withered, there was flesh holding out the skin. But there was an unhealthy puffiness, a loss of texture; not the grey look of death's proximity, but the loss of firmness associated with a laggard bloodstream. The heart is weary, Minn thought. She said, "You haven't had an easy life."

Gertrude looked up from her knitting abruptly. There was to be no talk of her personal life.

Minn backed down. "I guess I was jealous of Annie, but no more than I would have been of any other sister. She was sweet, wasn't she, a gentle little four-year-old all her life? Louisa's terribly like her."

81

"Where's Norman now?" Gertrude asked.

"Far East. Nepal. Katmandu."

Gertrude sniffed. She saw no vision of dyes and amber, men mounting mountain-tops. "He shouldn't leave you alone."

"He has no choice."

"It's not good for the children when the mother gets over-tired. You ought to have help."

"I wish I had. What's the news around here?"

"Nothing much. Tom Moore's Reeve of the township, that's a change. There's a new man for mayor, I don't know him."

"I notice there are houses by the creek."

"And more fools they. Your uncle Peter had a house there sixty years ago and had to leave it, it flooded in spring."

"Is Morgan still on the paper?"

"I wouldn't know, Minn, I wouldn't know. Since Mr Patterson died I don't hear the news from downtown any more. There's a new minister over from Belfast."

She didn't think she had the strength to go into that. "How's Annabel doing?"

"She's an excellent doctor. She always asks after you. She'll be surprised when I tell her you're having your fourth. When's it due?"

"June the eighth."

"In my day we told the doctor when we thought we were expecting and that was all. Does your back ache?"

"My feet swell."

"I hope you're not taking extra medicines."

"Just vitamins."

The clock on the mantelpiece — brass Corinthian columns, marble Ionian columns, lion masks, rings, and a surprising effeminate tinkle — struck four. Minn couldn't think of anything more to say. She waited for Gertrude to say something. She waited a long time. She thought of the time when in a waft of sentiment she had taken Louisa to see Annie in the Church Home, where they had reluctantly sent her because her kidney condition necessitated help they could no longer afford. Before a shocked attendant Minn put Louisa in Annie's arms, and Annie crooned and cradled her. "Pretty dolly," said Annie, "and Minnie has a pretty dress." Annie was grizzled and fifty and shot Minn looks of such love that the purity of it was frightening, and Minn began to cry, and reached for Louisa because Annie was losing interest and beginning to hold her by the leg.

Finally, she said, "The house looks nice, Mother."

"It needs painting. Alice keeps on at the garden. She has a wonderful green thumb."

"I'm glad to see you both so active. After Annie died . . . "

Gertrude stopped her with a look again. There was another silence divided between the clock and the knitting needles. Gertrude said, finally, "Mrs Dalgety at the library was asking for you."

"That's nice." Trying and failing to put a face on Mrs Dalgety.

"Orla Beavis is taking us out for dinner."

"I was just thinking of going."

"There's a cold roast Alice has. You could stay the night. It's a long drive."

Overnight. Climbing down the trees outside Pollyanna's window to have a baby on the sidewalk in front of the cigar store at midnight in defiance of the medical proximity of Annabel, in memory of Mr Punch. The bag of waters drooling "Mr Daniel looks like a spaniel" on the sidewalk, the night stores dreaming. One light over a shop and the night-policeman walking. While Bennie and Til writhe captive behind Annie's stainless-steel bars. "No," she said, "they wouldn't settle." She poured another cup of tea for her mother and said, "I'll see how they are in the kitchen."

They were all at the kitchen table and all covered with home-made jam. Alice was looking happy in a daft and haggard way, with one hand tickling Louisa, with another feeding Ben snips off the roast while he barked like a trained seal. Til slid to the floor and took the breadknife with her. Minn got it away from her and resurrected her, screaming. "You're both looking well," she said to Alice, parting Ben from a bottle of geriatric vitamins.

"We aren't what we were," said Alice. "But we're better off than some. They're dying like flies around us. Mr Patterson, Mrs Slattery. Isabel Cameron last week."

"I'm sorry."

"Your mother's got bad arthritis, but Annabel says she's as well as can be expected."

"And how are you?"

"Oh," she shrugged, "I'm like the river, I go on forever. It's in our family. Goodness, Minnie, he's eaten a button."

Ben was a good invention, Ben had taste. Minn grabbed him and held him by the feet, stuck her finger up his throat and pried around his tonsils. He coughed out the button, and some spit and some blood because she hadn't cut her fingernails, and he bit her finger, hard. The button he had swallowed was a wide-eyed bone waist-button. Alice stood up and sat down and stood up again, reached over to soothe him. "My, aren't you quick, though," she said.

"Shut up, Ben, it's your own fault," Minn said, while Alice winced for him. She got up and got the dishcloth and did their faces. Then she took Louisa upstairs.

My daughter in my house. When they die the church gets it for a parking lot. Mother's bed, ship of state. Telephone beside it now silent. Sewing room where Father's study was. Alice's little cell. White towels in the bathroom, still. Colours are vulgar and their purpose is to disguise dirt.

While Louisa piddled she looked in the medicine cabinet again. A caked tin of pine bathsalts from sacred Eaton's, a bottle of green soap. She pinched the little tin of nail-rouge and knew they'd notice, put it back again.

Alice had made up sandwiches, Gertrude had found or finished a pair of bow-legged soakers. Gertrude looked critically at the children. Ben grabbed her around the leg and bit her knee. Surprisingly, she smiled. "Let us know when you have the baby," she said.

When are you going to have the baby? A voice spoke from a long way off. She pulled herself back, awake again.

It was the cat-eyed anti-feminist. She closed her eyes again. "June," she said. "Early in June, if it holds."

"Is it your first?"

"God, no. Haven't you seen the upstairs?"

"Oh, it's your house. I thought it was a theatre party."

"It is and it isn't. Can I get you another drink?"

"No, I've had enough." She was right, her voice was thick and her face was blotchy. "I can't see a girl like you siding with the feminists."

"Can I bum a cigarette?"

"Sure, but I'm out of matches."

Minn rummaged in her pockets and found a folder. They lit up. "I'm not for them," she said, "I'm not against them. I hate arguments."

"But what are you going to tell your daughters?"

"What do you tell yours . . ."

"Well, Linda's fourteen, and Christy . . ." she was off. I've done it to people too, Minn thought, and let her go. Strange, intense woman. Turn those yellow eyes on kids and drive them . . . Balzac story, *Girl with the Golden Eyes*. Lesbian story, but very beautiful. Women fifty years behind men coping with homosexuality. That voice. If I were her daughter . . .

"Well, what do you think?"

"I think it's funny about Ziggy."

"Ziggy who?"

"A friend of mine called Ziggy. He wrote a zoological best-seller on the inequality and unreliability of women."

"So what's funny about it."

"I had a feeling it was aimed at me."

"Egotistic, aren't you? No daughter of mine is . . ."

Minn had a strong sudden desire to stand and stretch and beat her much-touted forty inches of breast and recite the beautiful Welsh rant that Hooper taught, that began, "Ruin seize thee, ruthless king, confusion on thy banners wait . . ." The education system can't have been as bad then as they say, she thought, if there were so many good lines in it. "Let's go and get ourselves another drink," she said. If we have to be buddies . . .

Even though half the guests had gone, the house still seemed to be bursting with people. Drop out of the city, move. Damn covetous eyes always on Mother's house. No, get a cabin, some land, some goats. Own cheeses. Who can't stand the stink of a ripe Camembert. "Bien fait, madame?" "Qui s'abandonne." In France there was the language and the food. Great film maker exiled by his own gluttony. Had a mind, an education, a gut. Years I spent waiting for him in the rue Dragon, he'd lounge in and say, "We're going to Parma to eat ham and violets." When I argued about his movies, he said I was a snob, a post-Santayana puritan. Gertrude never let me have saddle shoes.

Now or never, return to the land. Put up berries in brandy. Stout snakes-and-ladders fence around the garden. Who'll work the posthole-digger, who'll pay the man? Quick, come, Ben's in the bears . . .

She asked for a small drink, the waiter gave her a very big one. She handed it back and lauded herself for her courage. Glass in hand, the yellow-eyed lady disappeared. The waiter handed her back a watery drink. "Just about over now," she said. The waiter shrugged. He was dark and heavy-set, Mediterranean. Starting at the bottom. Greek? Portuguese? She wondered how much Reiner would pay him.

A woman was going out. High shoulders and funky lacquered hair. The kind of artificial silk that stinks of perspiration when you iron it.

The waiters were rinsing glasses at the kitchen sink, stacking them in the rental cases. The tramping on the worn protesting stairs was increasing. Soon her bed would be clear of coats. She wondered where to put herself until they were gone — it could not last much longer; she lingered alone in the back dining-room where the bar was and with one eye saw Honeyman staring flaccidly at her from his poster, with another Marvella and Oliver sneaking

86

out the back door, holding hands. Like a pair of gilded lizards. Their green eyes.

She held up her glass to Honeyman, since no one was there. "To male chauvinism," she said, and swallowed. It was awful, it was weak. She added a little more to it, guiltily, to colour up the water. "To female chauvinism," she said. She added some more. "Norman has some very funny things he says about you," she said. "When I'm looking big and tough he calls me 'Honeyman's Little Bit of Fluff.' There's also a gargling song he sings when the road is rough. It goes 'Honeyballs, Honeyballs, Honeyballs!' rising a half-tone like a doorbell." She heard herself and put her glass down. It wouldn't do to get drunk. It went with the country but not with the job she did.

Commotion at the door. Latecomers trampling on leavers. Who?

A girl shrieked, "My foot!" A man laughed a deep laugh she had heard before.

Minn went to the door. She was lunged at, lifted, swung: "Minnie!"

"Cal, forgod*sake*!"

"Excuse me, ma'am." He said it in a dreadful accent.

After all, it was good to see him. Not anyone you would look forward to, but the longevity of acquaintance . . .

"God, woman, it's good to see ya."

He was taller than his father, six feet two or three. He had the same long, loose-jointed half-ugly face, but his eyes blazed a different blue.

He had his big hick blue-denim arms around her and he was burrowing into her, leaning over her belly. She let herself sink into him for a moment, because his length and his body were good, but she gave nothing up to him. Honeyman had sent him to her for holidays from his English schools, and his New England schools, and she had pushed him uncertainly through a term at the Alliance Francaise; she knew him. While he was embracing her, he was gesturing to someone for a drink with one of his knuckly hands. She disengaged herself and pulled him into the the living room.

He had people with him who gave her hope: a girl six feet tall with an Afro haircut and a face with feeling in it, a willowy simple-faced man with something good in his eyes. The man wearing a patchwork velvet vest. "Hi," she said to them, making her voice melting and American.

She looked at Cal, holding him at arm's length, knowing he liked it. "You look wonderful," she lied.

"Aw, Minn." Cowboy accent coy down to the boots. "And ain't Trawna gettin' to be a great place?"

Johnny Cash, with just a *soupçon* of Proust.

The man in the velvet vest was looking hopeful and holding the guitar. Reiner appeared with three glasses of bourbon.

If you don't play the game there's no game. "Play me something," Minn said. Looking at him, thinking, I'm not going to like what Ben is . . .

"Wrote a new one t'other day," he said. "Called it Ol' Granny Gin Ain't Gonna Get Me by The Shoulder. Wanna hear it?"

The room had coagulated around him. Velvet-vest handed him his guitar. At least he can play his own, she thought.

He straightened out in the approved spineless posture between the coffee table and the sofa. He fiddled with the knobs on the guitar. He thumped the wood, he crooned.

Minn turned to the tall girl. "Where do you come from?"

"Now, Minnie," Cal said, "keep your trap shut, I'm singin' you a free song."

Ol' Granny Gin had to be a put-on, but he did it well. It struck Minn that the guitar was a long way from piano lessons but they still had to put their hands on you when they taught you, and how had Cal learned? Watching his daddy's westerns?

He finished. He pulled her over and patted her ass. "Barefoot in the winter, pregnant in the summer," he said. Her eyes rolled back, his father used to say that, but she caught them. "Sure, boy."

"How're the little ones? Let's git 'em down. I haven't seen none of them but the girl-child. Hey, Fred!"

It sounded like a compromise between a panty-raid and a game of Red Rover. She said fiercely, "Where're you playing, Cal?"

"Just finished Buffalo, doin' the Riverboat. Hey, let's get those kids down here."

"Not at two in the morning, Cal."

"Hell it ain't two ..." He looked at his watch, at her ... "Well, if you say so, Minnie." To the others, "She was always a hard, hard woman."

How much older was she? Fifteen, sixteen years? No, ten, ten exactly. That mess of a kid and his holidays and not knowing what to do with him, and him bringing his friends to the flat Honeyman said she couldn't bring her friends to. The money, the effort to swing.

"You know," he said, "I was in the bin last year?"

"What bin?"

"The Upper New York State Fancy Fancy Bin. For trying to knife a guy under the influence. I come a long way since then, Minn."

"I'm glad you came as far as Toronto."

"Aw, nothing, nothing. I came to work and Reiner he called me."

She was sitting beside him now, feeling sorry for him. That awful western accent that was no real part of him. My old friend. He said, "You're gittin to be a big woman, Minn."

"That's what they say, Cal."

"Well, you can't be a movie star forever, heh? You oughta bring those tads out to the ranch, sometime, Minn."

"Where's the ranch?"

"You oughta come out and live with us out in Denver where the air is clean."

"They make poison gas in Denver."

"Well, they gotta make it somewhere, don't they?"

She did not leap to the fly. She found herself snuggling to him. He said, "I was thinking about my Daddy tonight, Minn."

Her instinct was to say, "Oh, I wouldn't do that." She kept her mouth tight shut. "I guess he was a good man," he said.

89

"He sure was, Cal." And damn me for catching the accent.

"That's what we say about people when they're dead, isn't it?"

"Sure, Cal."

"Well, wasn't he a good man, Minn?" The voice rose dangerously in the nostrils.

"Sure, he was a good man, if you want to make it that simple."

"We've all got a little sin in us, eh?" he rolled his eyes unattractively sideways and dug her belly with his elbow. The baby kicked.

"He was a honey," she said. "I never knew anybody to be so good to me."

His shoulders sloped, he relaxed. "He sure was a hell of a good man."

"And so are you, baby."

The lights were too bright. Hundreds of watts were burning. She got up to extinguish the dining-room. He followed her. "Whatcha living here for, now? Whatcha doing in the city?" He picked up his guitar and slung it over his shoulder and in the same motion waved his glass towards Reiner's waiting bourbon bottle. It was filled. "Whatcha living here for? It's not healthy. Why doncha come out and live with me in Denver?"

"Norman works here."

"Well, screw Norman. He's never home, is he? I haven't been to this house but once that he was here. Those little kids can't hardly know him."

"I know him, Cal."

"And those little kids could be runnin' in the country . . . "

"How's Mary-Ann?"

"She left me. She up and left me."

"They do that sometimes, boy."

He sat down again, dangled his hands from his wrists between his legs. "I give her a bad time, Minn, and once she had me in that institution she left me."

She sat quietly beside him, trying to think, is there something I should say, or is the stranger riding in from the

90

west and doing his bit? He had gone into himself a little. She looked up at his six-foot friends. Their faces urged her to handle him. "It's all right, Cal," she said.

"I mean that about the ranch; if things git bad, you come out there with them."

"Sure, Cal. I'd love to, Cal."

Reiner spoke: "And now we are all going to Luba's. I hope you can come, Minn."

"No, love. I can't leave them alone with the hippies."

Cal sprang to life. "I could baby-sit."

She laughed. "To hell with you. Go on to Luba's." His friends relaxed.

He said, "Guinèvre's out there too. I'd like to see you together."

Because he expected it, "Why, Cal?"

"Cause once when I was a little kid travelling with my mother, I saw in a barbershop window in South Dakota a black widow spider and a yellow jacket both in one bottle. It was a fine thing to see."

"Good-bye, Cal."

"You think about Denver, now."

"I'll think about Denver. Come over for a meal. Come over and see the kids."

"Fred and Isa and I will be over tomorrow to have a look at those kids."

"Nice of you, Cal. Love to Luba, Reiner."

She leaned against the door-jamb, enjoying a surge of weak pathos. The two bus-boys, now looking like sinister grown-ups instead of aged elves (they had removed their green spencer jackets) nudged her gently as they moved the booze and the mix and the fancy cutting boards and ice buckets and the crumpled linen out. In the blackness she could hardly see to wave at Calvin's car.

9

Mrs N.R. Burge, 37, of 26 Bute Place in the inner core of the city was arrested at 3 p.m. Friday by officers of the Domestic Morality Squad and charged with failing to keep an orderly house.

Squad Chief William R. Trotter, who last month left an important private post to head this major new Metro department, stated that this was the Squad's first arrest.

"Our aim," he said, "is to start people thinking clean by forcing them to be clean." He added that meticulous attention is being paid by the squad to core areas of Toronto, where there is considerable crowding and domestic discouragement. "Middle-class values have got to be imposed in order to get these girls to clean up," he said. He designated Mrs Burge's house as a distressed area and said he would call it privately a pig-sty. Samples of dirt on upstairs windowpanes were found by Squad inspectors to contain jam, plasticene, Cheez-Whiz, peanut butter and human excrement, and there was a pubic hair in the bathtub. A garbage bag was overturned on the kitchen floor and there was evidence that one child had been eating a mixture which contained honey and hair.

As she departed to the Don Jail to await trial, Mrs Burge waved a tearful farewell to Louisa, 4, and twins Benny and Tilly, 2. "I know it's for the good of other people that I'm being made an example of," she said, "but it's hard to take at my advanced age." She stated also that she felt that neither the insect situation nor the fungoid growth under the kitchen linoleum were her responsibility, since they had been there when she moved into the house, and fumigation of a property this size was too large an expense for the average downtown family. She continued, "There's a pubic hair in the bathtub in Virginia Woolf's

The Years, *a book her husband Leonard was not fond of,*
but I can't cite the page. It's something that happens as you
get older." She fell into a deep sleep in the back of the
police car.

Mr Trotter, who at 22 is considered one of the most
brilliant young men ever to interest himself in municipal
politics, shook his head in bewilderment. "I can't believe it.
What does she do with her time? I've seen Polacks keep a
better house than that, and she's the daughter of a former
premier of Ontario."

In Magistrate's Court next morning, Mrs Burge said
that she would try to do better if the house was fumigated.
She pointed out to Magistrate Grungeon that the house was
of the same vintage as the City Hall where court was held
and asked if he had noticed that the linen wallpaper of this
courtroom was decorated with rare art-nouveau stringwork
of a water-lily pattern.

Magistrate Grungeon sentenced her to the rest of her
life at 26 Bute Place, which its owner, Mrs Betty-Ann Peel,
said she could not afford to fumigate at present mortgage
rates, especially when the tenants were two days behind
with their rent and appeared to give large parties. Magistrate Grungeon ordered D.M. Squad inspectors to supply
Mrs Burge with a can of sheep dip and a spray gun. Mrs Burge
was led away bulging.

Ooze on the ozite, bugs in the swag, house looming.
How shall we live now, Mother?

She surfaced from sleep. There's the church, there's
the steeple. The people have all gone home.

I own myself again, she thought. I've been returned.
I'm somewhat overdue, there was a fine, but I'm here
again.

Party. Smarty-smarty gave a . . . nobody came to Scott
Fitzgerald's birthday. There were people here, a lot of
people. But a great veil between me and them, a fog, a
thickness.

Funny to see Sam. Thought I knew him. I went out with Ziggy, but I liked Sam, he was easier to be with. Three of us were buddies. Times have changed, lady.

Cal. Cal. Used to be pathetic, now he's merely unreal. Don't believe in the ranch in Denver. Anybody who invites a woman and four kids to stay has to be lying. Honeyman didn't leave him much. He picked up the western accent at the movies, watching television. Hasn't been west of Chicago since he was ten, he would have told me. *Dear surrogate mum* . . . Me and my daddy, the dream that never came off for him. Ever since kids found out they were supposed to be loved, they've been screaming for more. That pimply kid Cal pretending to be Holden Caulfield; steaming around Paris complaining about the plumbing and looking for hotdogs. Seven thousand boarding schools. Psychiatrists. Trouble. Honeyman laying aside the letter, sighing, "Cal again." Mother was some kind of society bitch. Or was she?

Seems remote, now. Everything's remote, glazed.

Always the same questions come: what is right? what is real?

What is real is what noses up to you, winds around your neck refusing to let go. Sixteen and twenty-six besieging thirty-six — lying, that's interesting. I skipped a birthday — twenty refusing to clothe itself and appear. What's right is another question. Mothers are invariably wrong.

She rubbed her belly and that was real. And right. Wished Norman would come home and make her self real. The baby still kicked and jerked. Another go-all-day-resist-sleep-zonk-collapse one. He'd fit with the others. They were real. Home was real.

The house was all-too-real. Once they gutted and replastered it like the others in the row, what would it be? All smart with hard outlines, without its fancy woodwork, its plaster ornaments? Well, clean. What's real, sir?

Something touched by hands, something made, human, humanised, not sterile, not plasticised.

Upstairs, now. She heaved herself up the first step by tugging at the newel post, stood stock still, listened. By the

94

pricking of my . . . wouldnitbewonderfulif? The beginning, the drumroll, *Roll on thou deep and dark blue Ocean, roll/ Ten thousand ships roll over thee in vain* . . . the first of them.

She waited. Another did not come.

Damn. Get it over, now.

No, be patient. Leave the seeds in the hotbed, if you transplant them too soon they'll be weak little things.

But that dark roll. Sensation she had forgotten, something magnificent, grand about it. It rings in the ears. Not like the late sharp painful ones, electric shocks, worrying, but first dungeon-dark quakings, the machine trying itself out. Not surprised if it came a little early. No, too soon to hope. No flesh on the child yet, no antibodies built.

But the roll, the power of it. A transsensual thing: you heard it as well as felt it, assigned colour to it.

And what was good about the power was that it was in you but not of you, not belonging to your will or your ego, something independent, something grander than will: standing on the cliffs over the lake unprotected from the storm watching the breakers and the fat rain trying to flatten the breakers. Something Lawrence should have had and would have understood — and romanticised, wouldn't he, though? — the grandeur of being operated from within-without. The poem about the gentians. Dark blue furred vagina-flower.

Sobering, sobering. False labour, but still felt. Sitting on the steps passively, waiting to be entertained by the seismic shuddering.

No. It isn't going to come. No thunder, blankness. Up to pee, then. The baby's still, now. Lulled by that power?

In my government there'd be compulsory downstairs bathrooms for all mothers, and a squad of government housekeepers on motorcycles, old women who'd flap in, pounce on the children, crying, "I love this one, oh, isn't that one wonderful, can I have them for a day, the darlings?" holiday help by lottery, abortion on demand, cheap nationalised shoes. In my government . . .

Down again, she picked up glasses idly, carried them to the kitchen. Rinsed, stacked them in rental cases.

Emptied a million ashtrays into a plastic bag, rinsed them, scraped at the tar with her thumbnail, stacked them. Wondered about Reiner, what made him tick besides ambition. Poured herself the heel of the Scotch bottle, only a little one, saw Reiner sucked into the maw of an inflatable sofa, babies floating in the sky on them ...

The mind has molehills and they lead to tunnels of escape.

Out of this skin, this house, this country, even. Why and where? Up in the thin air with Norman how should I breathe? He rolls in madder-root and the tender leaves of tea, shouting "Because it's there!" Hairless women pelt him with coral and amber, crones carrying unbrellas on their heads salute him, he is borne through the market past dun weathered wooden porticos, robed in saffron, turbanned in purple. A girl with great dark serious eyes puts gold in his nose. Around him the mountains rise in perpetual erection. He floats in Mogul patternings, he is rubbed in yak butter, he sits obedient winding their rough-dyed wool.

And up in the attic, in Oliver's studio, all over this town, they are searching for him. The peasant is the city-dweller's dream. They are casting off Bauhaus, seeking the miraculous texture of the dying trees.

Back home there was Mrs Heber, whom Alice was kind to, an English warbride who had no front teeth and two half-witted children. "She was on the stage," said Alice, half thrilled and a little ashamed of herself, "she was a chorus girl, but her looks are gone now, poor dear." Taking her another apple pie.

And Marvella? A new breed, or exotic by my ignorance of her? Stealing my spoons, and where's the pierced sugar-shaker Aunt Em sent me? Beautiful tonight, subterranean: through the silver lace the little titties shaking. Meatless fingers. Oddly like Oliver, same size, same sallow colour. Twenty years between them, but he is small, unwithered. Wicked to let them run off together, malicious to envisage Jane-Regina torn from her helpmeet. But they go well together, green lizards with enamel eyes ...

She brought a tray for more glasses, and, thinking "Lizards", banged it hard on the dining-room table, looked up towards the front room, and was amazed. It was not her house, it was her mother's house: Turkey carpet, plants in the window, dark curtains. Only the piano missing.

She sank into herself, startled. Did she so much love Gertrude that she made her house again? Was she like her, staunch, starched, domineering, hiding all hurt? It has to be done, it *shall* be done: and firm feet approaching. Were the children wild because she refused to be Gertrude?

Cal, tonight, then. Sitting close beside him. Getting, giving a little: but stone-walling him and he knew it. He went to Luba's because she was not giving herself to his fantasies, not child to his grown-up, but mother. Offering the bait of Denver (even if there was no Denver) and withdrawing it through Guinèvre: because she was grown up and away from him, too old to play games, too steady, too unwilling.

Lord, let there be no more festivals. Tonight was enough. I do not love the blow-up of Honeyman on the wall. Those eyes are closed now, and I am another person. Young Cal no more the distressed teen-ager, Paris another town. The Royale is Le Drug-Store. Honeyman is dead. Godard is the great film maker, soon to be superceded. Let the world move on.

But clearing glasses from the mantlepiece she found Reiner's folder and looked at the photograph of Honeyman and read the pseudo-scholarly text. God, they were making cult-figures as fast as they could find them, had Christianity gone out for film-worship? The man was a craftsman, knew what to do with a frame, how to build a sequence, but he wasn't Leonardo. The airs and graces they gave him he would have laughed at. What he wanted was money for a villa behind Cannes. What he loved were the blossoming dry Midi hills, like California, but with castles and good cheeses in them, best of both worlds. He made pot-boilers at Cinecittà and Westerns in Hollywood. It was a job, a thing he did, man. He crafted it, but he didn't open it up at the end, he wasn't an artist, he was only interested in the finite. He said he knew his limitations. He said the ones who thought they were artists always got in trouble. All he wanted was to do a good job and eat well, he said.

All? How did she know? It was long ago and she was young, then, Marvella's age, out to conquer the world and equal to anything even . . .

Sitting in a tower in a little walled town near Marseilles, having parted from the boy who was driving her from Ibiza to Paris (he and his friends were called beatniks but they were also research psychologists on holiday) because he was fed up with sightseeing and she wasn't. He said, "Get out, then," and she did, proudly, and marched through the city gate. Two small travellers' cheques in her wallet and the rest of her money in Paris, and how do you get out of here?

The town was lovely, intact within bastioned walls. You could climb over anything, there were no guides or guidebooks. When she was tired she sat down to read (she had left her suitcase at a *pension*) in a corner of a watchtower, close by the stairs, so the sun shaded her book (*The Quest for Corvo*). A black scorpion crept out of a crack near her, and she watched it. Then a shadow fell and a huge American-shod foot stumbled over her, a hand came down, she said "Watch the scorpion," and she knew the huge length of Honeyman.

She thought, now, that it must have been good for him, to meet someone who knew nothing about him and cared less and wanted only to be twenty and explore the world. He was willing to help.

He had just brought the unit down to the town (Dead Egg, he called it), the actors weren't here yet, his business was quickly over with the scenarist (he worked fast, Honeyman, he was always sure of what he wanted). The movie they were to make was Italian, a sex-and-saints job. The place was perfect for it, it was used a lot for pictures about the crusades. Had she seen that other tower? Out that slot they had poured the boiling oil. Had she seen around the neighbourhood?

He was from, originally, Nebraska. Via Princeton. He had got into film-making from something else, writing perhaps, or horse-breaking. He liked horse-operas, he said, because it was all there for you and you made the picture around it. He'd done a lot of them in California. "Made a lot of pictures, made a lot of dough," she could hear his voice. "Got tired of the rat-race once the television slump set in. Wives, worry, alimony, kids. Like it here, now."

He was colloquial, and, on the surface, so very much like a smooth simple movie hero that she fell in love with him. He saw it, and was gentle. He said, "I like you too, kid." They drove around the delta, where there were rice paddies now that the *colons* were back from Viet Nam. He drove her to Arles, Nîmes, Avignon. He found she liked to eat, so they went places to eat together. Once the picture started she lived on olives during the day to make her money last. He got her a costume and put her in a shot. He laughed at her a lot. He said she couldn't move, walked like a sailor, what the hell kind of shoes had her mother kept her in, but it was OK if she sat or stood or ran.

Used to call her "Honeyman's Klootch."

When work on the film got serious he put her on the train at Nîmes, gave her the key to his flat in Paris. In the rue Dragon. Use it, he said, but don't let anybody else in. I'll see you in a month, enjoy yourself.

She was with him, on and off, for five or six years. With him, or under his aegis, alternately shattered by his absence or obsessed by his presence.

She was his girl he took to small, secret, delicious places to eat, his secret girl. There was a leggy skinny blonde he took to the *Tour d'Argent*.

The trouble began when she became dissatisfied with being a tenth of a grain of his life, and knowing he was the whole of hers, starting wanting to marry him. "They all do," he said. Then she turned into a maenad, spat fire. And one day at the hairdresser in St Germain des Prés where they do your hair with a little hand-blower, and four girls comb, she opened *Elle* and saw a feature on him and Guinèvre his French fiancée, and fainted.

Any other girl, he pointed out, would have got off her ass and made an actress of herself. God bless her, she hadn't. But wasn't a work permit in Paris, a flat in the rue Dragon (around the corner from Lipp, and she saw Sartre there once, really, the culture hero) wasn't what she had had — wild boar in Yugoslavia, lasagna in Bologna, roe deer in Versailles with him, wasn't that . . . something?

He was kind to her, fatherly. She made an execrable scene, and he took it well, the storm of tears, the shouting, the curse upon him. But he was tired of having his public and private lives divided, he was in love with this woman Guinèvre, who had left her husband for him, and had a villa at Cannes.

So for five years she lived and breathed Honeyman and saw him perhaps ten weeks a year, was his private and humble friend. And when she packed and left the rue Dragon (around the corner from St Germain des Prés, close to Flore and Deux Magots and Lipp but in fact when she was not working she stayed in the flat and read and ate yoghurt and little goats' cheeses that smelled like farts, bought at Monoprix; and went to movies) she thought she would die of unhappiness, and discovered, after a month's hunching past cinema marquees and moping around the barricades of that year's revolution, that nobody noticed, that she did not in fact die, that she liked people, people her own age, as he had said she would.

More to it than that, of course; life for her was always rich as a pudding. She had a few friends and the few friends branched into more, an accretion that started with people she met in the studios and more who joined their table at the Dome, at the Coupole, even at the Closerie de Lilas where they engaged in Hemingway worship. And then Norman who stopped her in the Old Navy (when they weren't working they were always in cafés) and said knew her, she was Lizzie Borden and Esther M. Williams, sure she was. She liked him immediately, he had what she responded to in men, vitality.

What a good rich life it was, then, when you were young and had a Honeyman, and could walk into Paris offices and come out employed, dubbing, translating, re-writing a script, holding a pile of props at the edge of a set. It was no small thing to be equipped to survive.

And there was the love.

She thought a lot about love now that she had children. She wondered how so many people could be so wrong about it, how they could say there were so many sorts of it, and there seemed to be only one, a well of feeling in the back of your personality, in the bowels of your personal earth: you tended your supply carefully, tried to get in order later to be able to give, for it worked better when it was primed, but it was all the same stuff: the kids seething like insects in the playroom and Minn sitting mending just outside the gate so they wouldn't grab the wool away, and love shining like the sun. It was like being in bed with Honeyman, when "Thy belly is a sheaf of wheat" led to stories of his father's farm and of her uncle's farm, and the harvesting and the threshing, and a young lurch into Paris in search of apple pie. And often love was so transparent you didn't know it was there, it existed also as general goodwill and enthusiasm, and a grey day came when it was gone, and you knew what it had been yesterday.

She sat with her back very straight on the bottom step and without the courage to go up alone to bed.

10

Clock nags; make, then, the chatelaine's tour: back door and front, dining-room window. Taps off securely, butter covered away from beasts. Upstairs, cover them. Two on their backs, flushed. Til gat-toothed, delicious, a bawd, a strumpet. Ben sopping. Sleeps on his knees. Turn, stretch, lad. Too sleepy you are, to kick. Smell of wet pee-cloth, taste of nickel-plated pins. Times we've rushed him to Mordie for objects ingested. Psyche plans accidents, reacts in panic to reality. Get out of this house soon. Need neighbours, grass. Respectable children are run over by Eaton's trucks, not wholesale poulterers'. Like best, Sundays down here. *Terrains-vagues,* empty offices and factories, roads littered with gaskets, the building you never see on weekdays that looks like a fortress in Khartoum. Lazing across streets like fat cats. Going down to the siding where they load the paper, letting them run on the platform. Big Ben-sized bolts. Hanging over the railway bridge. World all our own. Deep in begonias we'll miss this. There's a real estate place advertising houses, expensive, children welcome. What'd he say if he came back and found us gone? LOST: One family. Weight slides off the shoulders, queasiness of sense of loss is quickly comforted. Have to buy a lawn-mower.

There, boy, that's right, sleep. Tomorrow's another, and all yours. Here's your blocks in with you, better than stripping wallpaper, playing with home-made plasticene. Feet out of your sleepers, lad? Spring's here, never mind.

What are they dreaming, what are their fantasies? Up in the attic in Godwin robins throbbed in the daylight-saving dusk, I day-dreamed, then I slept. Child's dreams of notoriety: the best whistler in the world, the ethereal ballet dancer, even — and it was carved pearwood, polished, smooth, round grain following the curve of the cheeks, beautiful, entire, and fitted together in two halves with a wooden peg — The Only Girl with The Wooden Bum. It hurt their hands when they spanked me, and it was a circus living. They came from miles around to see me. Little Minnie, the Eighth Wonder of the World.

Little new one, hold your hour if you can. It's a long life, and a devious psychology you're facing. You'll be more theirs than mine, running always with the pack. You'll mope when they go to school. And face a dying world. Never mind, we'll give you rose-hip syrup for your vitamins, and gripewater with fine engraved labels, and find you a summer wilderness to hide in. Strengthen your legs to run away with, God help you.

She passed her own door, saw her bed clear of coats now, still heaped with books and an ashtray. Thought, Louisa if she's bright will wear a blazer that says "Class of 1984".

102

Not safe to wonder what kind of world it will be then, she thought. And, knowing she should go to bed, unwilling to go to bed, she idled in the corridor, half-yawning. Would she sleep if she lay down? If she stayed up any longer she would be cross with them to-morrow, the long lug up the stairs with them would be intolerable, she would lose her temper but . . .

She went downstairs, got a pack of cards out of the sideboard, laid out a solitaire, thinking, jack, queen, king, generations, interior landscapes, theirs, ours. Gene Autry, Roy Rogers, Sonja Henie. Alice and Gertrude laughing at Amos and Andy. Talk of Marie Dressler. The first television that came to Godwin: Joe McCarthy with five o'clock shadow interrogating, accusing. In a furniture store window. Grey airwave invasion unwilled. My country tis of theirs.

And will Marvella sing to her grandchildren about Mr Kite?

She slapped and shuffled. The cards whispered gotobed, gotobed. Some people are called that, Gotobed. No. You have to live each night as if there will never be another one.

She put the cards away and took out her other toys.

Mrs MacGregor at home had had a pair of Silent Companions, and perhaps she needed them. They were her household gods, a pair of Georgian fire-screens, simulacra of liveried servants, a capped elegant housemaid bearing a tray, a wigged serving-man. Hers were three-quarter scale and immensely valuable. The fire was never lit behind them lest they burn, there was fuss about the climate's warping them. Minn had always had the impression that when she was alone after Annabel went to bed Mrs MacGregor talked to them. Certainly when she went up to her room for her long dying, and disgusted Annabel and Dr MacGregor by refusing to be hospitalised, she took them with her, sweet vapid faces like her own or General Wolfe's, a conceit in Gainsborough colours. There had been a vogue for them once, in England, during an antique servant shortage.

Minn's too derived from the erstwhile mother country, from the toyshop she and Norman haunted in Seven Dials, buying not for prospective children but because they were each other's children. These were two-inch cardboard toy-theatre characters which were manipulable on wire slides like extended paper-clips; they wore Chinese costume for Ali Baba (the English, it seemed to her, had been well served by their muddy and undiscriminating minds: with every non-islander a wog, what does it matter if you mix their styles?), their waistcoats extended in pagoda skirts. She had made these up last summer when Norman was in Brasilia, and been ashamed to show them to him in case he thought her silly.

She had worked hard on them, sorting and clipping photographs to match the tiny scale of their faces, so that now Ali Baba was Churchill, a wonderful figure if you considered that for the last ten years of his life he was obviously stuffed, his hand raised artificially to the window and pulled by a pickled tendon into V-for-Victory, the way you manipulate a cut-off chicken's foot. The last obscene years in London justified, the sickening adulation put away. And Proust was happy in costume, the table was the beach at Cabourg, where they had never been. She had had to cut his face out of a library book with a razor blade and felt infinitely guilty about it, and liked him better for it: though he would never have stooped.

And she had made Gertrude-and-Alice-at-home out of a joined pair of courtesans, and a Paris Gertrude-and-Alice out of another. They stood gesturing and posturing, Nell Gwynn and Mrs Siddons and Rachel in their poses.

She had not made up their cardboard theatre. Norman had been planning to do it for years.

Nor had she made up Norman. She tried, but he didn't look right. He would not fictionalise. She replaced him with Disraeli, the best she could do. Poor Hemingway she couldn't put in oriental costume.

One of them was Honeyman, from one of Reiner's folders.

What she was trying to do was to create some kind of concrete landscape of her imagination, but she never succeeded at it. She took them out of their shoe-box and set them on the table sadly. She was not desperate enough to talk convincingly to them (without hearing her own voice in her ears and being shy of it) and they remained paper figures, flat, inaccurately cut, with small out-of-scale faces pasted on. Maybe if she went upstairs and got some pot they would look better, but she doubted it. Growing up in orthopaedic shoes and school uniforms and being fed shepherd's pie and Lancashire hot-pot kept her from flying. Their Lafcadio Hearn yellowness and their pagoda dresses confronted her and failed her. Stevenson had written movingly about playing with them, and she had hoped to play, to fly away on their backs to a personal never-never-land. All they had done was to teach her that she was one of the grown-ups at last.

She was beginning this baby when she made them. She had had a bad attack of *mishega* which frightened her. Mordie shook his head and gave her what the babysitter called "water pills" and said, "You're crazy to have another kid. You ought to take care of yourself." And when she cried brushed her shoulder, "I'm sorry, kid. We nearly lost you last time. You worry me." But failed to suggest an abortion.

Women's tension, water on the brain, water pills. Clinging to the idea of a large family, wondering what the hell a back-street abortionist would do with a Lippes loop. This time she ought to have a quiet Caesarean and get herself tied off. Only the fittest can reproduce from now on.

You thought, pregnant the first time, joy, Jemima Puddleduck with her brood trotting after her. You found they didn't. You had to force coherence on them, and if you were bad at that, stood on streetcorners in extravagant Noh-play postures, wondering which to rescue if at all . . .

I will look back on these years with considerable amusement, but it's a crazy way to live. Thought we were superior to live downtown, not in suburban little boxes: this is a big one. We live isolated, furious, alone in an urban desert. Paying for independence with hysteria. If there's no help we cannot kiss and part, we have to go slogging on.

105

And we have evenings to invent, and nights, being sleepless with the worry of it all.

She pushed Honeyman along the surface of the table, which was farther than she had pushed Honeyman in real life. They had to protect themselves against these women, men, and they all knew how. Honeyballs and his three apartments, and wasn't she lucky to draw the one on the rue Dragon and the education with it? Still. She smiled wanly at him. He knew her type. Barefoot in the winter, pregnant in the summer, and with a pair of hands itching to wrench the life out of a child. Lady with big ego seeks child with same. Gentleman with big ego seeks girl to feed with game. Where it gets you is here, trying to walk the narrow way between vitamin-deficiency and vitamin poisoning.

Funny she didn't have one of her father. There must be pictures around. The Honourable Gentleman in permanent eclipse. A vague memory of loving him as a child, before he disappeared into the maw of politics. Afterwards, he not only lived at Lucy's, he had a string of rural offices, practised different days in different villages — what did she know of him? Their intimate encounters had been few and furious.

She looked resentfully at the little figures. They would never dance under their Brighton parasols. They were no better than the pack of cards she had made with friends' faces on them, that would not shuffle and slide; they were boondoggle, an excuse for not sweeping down the stairs. You could attach fancy ideas to them — she had taken them through the Yeats-Charles Williams-Tolkien dance and come out to nothing on the other side — but in their cold little comfortless paper hearts they were nothing but the boondoggle of an idle procrastinating complaining woman in a dirty house. If she had had an open fire she would have swept them in.

Herself the rump-fed ronyon, Honeyman ready-steady-dead. The two Gertrudes and the two Alices a chapter in somebody else's history. Proust and Churchill and Disraeli, forgodsake!

106

She crammed them back in their box and got up to look out the window. There was a light rain falling, and she supposed bitterly that she could attach some significance to that to keep herself out of bed. Like standing remembering lugubrious nights in Paris, wandering past shuttered shop-fronts in the little streets that run down to the quais. And now it was a felony to take a step out of the house.

She felt someone behind her and turned. "What is it, Marvella?"

Marvella was dressed in jeans and a tee-shirt again. She stood lean as a snake, holding money out. "The rent."

"Well, goodness me, at this hour . . ." Minn stopped, ashamed of her peevish voice. "I'm annoyed with myself for not having gone to bed," she said. "I don't need that money this week: you can keep it if you help me with the children tomorrow."

"Why? Why won't you take it?" The girl had made a cult of expressionlessness before adults, but there was some kind of fear in her eyes now.

"I'm too tired to think about money."

"You were after me for it all last week."

"I'm sorry. I'll take it, then." She put it into her pocket. "I wish you'd help me tomorrow. It's late, now, and I know I won't sleep. I'll be desperate."

"I don't know if I'll be here. You can always get Richard."

Minn went on staring at her. She, too, was grey with fatigue, spun fine, living on a reserve that was running out fast. Damn you and your freedom that's killing you, Minn thought; we had to go abroad. She said, "I saw you with Mr Magill." and clapped her hand over her mouth in remorse.

Marvella did not move, but she widened her stare. There was no going back now so Minn said, "Tell me what he's like as a person, some day, if you feel like it. Good-night, child."

"Good-night, Mrs Burge."

Time stretches and snaps like a mile of elastic . . .
from a poem by Minn Williams, 11-B, appreciated by Minn
Williams alone.

She stood by the window a moment longer, then went back to her shoebox companions and thought, well, some women pot, and, if someone visiting the Tate could get me a postcard of The Death of Chatterton, I'd glue his face on the reclining Vizier. She made sure they were packed away uncrumpled and put them in a drawer.

I could read, or play bridge, she thought. I could take a course or go to meetings. I could paint, I could take up etching, I could get the television back. I could go to bed. I don't have to spend the small hours squeezing sores. She headed towards the stairs.

And found John Colebrook standing wistfully in the hall, wearing a dripping cape. "Don't go," he said, "show me your little people."

"You missed the party."

He put his hand on her shoulder and steered her. "Give us a drink and show us your little people."

If it seemed that they had known him always, it was because he was a member of a race. He was tall, diffident, destitute. He lived from drink to drink. And he was shy and broken but never quite as broken as she thought.

"You're sending out wonderful overtones of Aristide Bruant and decay," she said.

"I was just passing."

He was grey, he was sixty now. Boozing and cadging had not so much marked him as lightened him and made him frail; he was as light and leached as pumice. But the hard long winter had marked him this year. He stooped, now, his capillaries reached to breathe and left red webs upon his nose.

He had long hands, and had tried, once, to be a sculptor. She had met him in the Salvation Army book store. He knew about editions. He was English. Norman did not like him.

She got him the box of characters on slides. "I used to have these once," he said. She got him a beer. He thanked her for it and sipped it slowly. "You look tired," he said. "Are you sure that isn't an elephant you're carrying?"

"Yes."

"Tell me about Churchill being stuffed."

It had seemed a witty theory at the time, but she was too tired for cleverness now. Their relationship proceeded by means of small, elegant narrations strung between them like beads on a nerve. They would go on from Churchill to the Queen, who was essentially of Bone China, and invent dukes and duchesses to fit, if Norman wasn't home to be bored by it. He had not many facial expressions, something undignified had happened to his face in the war, but his hands, which could not sculpt, would fidget with excitement on the table, he would twist his turquoise ring and make a flourish. She saw him perhaps three times in a year, and late at night.

She went to the kitchen and brought back a basin and nail brush and clean linen huck towels from her mother's house, and went back for more beer. She pulled her chair close to his.

She did it properly, as if she were in the old house by starched curtains, placing a towel (yellowed in its folds) under the table under the basin, and another beside it, for his hands. He was passive. It was odd to handle a body that did not resist her. She picked up his hands as if they were separate from the rest of him, and put them in the basin and put lemon soap on them from her own hands. She thought, I would worry if the children were so obedient.

She dug hard into the lemon soap with the nail brush and scrubbed his knuckles. They were red and scabby from a winter without gloves. The veins were big and buckled. He had hang-nails on hang-nails. When he winced she went to get him another bottle of beer.

She scrubbed his ring carefully around the edges. Turquoise was soft as amber is. Once he took his left hand out and shook it over the towel, and swigged his bottled beer and gave the hand back to her again. She worked at the nails and knuckles, tickling and teasing his palms, chewing with the brush at his callouses, wondering how he got them without working. When she was finished there was grey scum on the water. Hands pink as Ben lay on the towel. He dried them himself.

"Do you do this often?" he asked.

She blushed, and dropped the brush. Went to slop the dirty water in the kitchen sink.

Do you do this often?

Occasions for touching: medical examinations, dressing, spanking, making love, pecking cheek, shaking hands, having coat put on, rocking children. "No," she said.

"That is, on the whole, wise."

"And you?"

"You've stripped off a year's protection against the weather. Have you something for that in the house?"

There was, she explained, a glaucous bum cream named for *lares et penates* and three bucks a tin that stained upholstery; and thrush cream, and impetigo cream and vaseline; cornflour and Lasar's paste that made her think of upending Lascars, and rosewater with glycerine, and honey-and-almond cream and cucumber lotion, the heel of a bottle, from France. She brought him a patent handlotion.

He desisted from cracking his knuckles. He sat and rubbed his hands and smiled at her.

Then she cleaned his nails and cut them, digging hard into the black quick, softening the grown cuticles. "You've got gentleman's hands," she said. "They're very beautiful."

He curled the ends of his fingers under as if to hide them.

He kept the nails of his little fingers long like a Levantine. For cleaning his ears? For his masculinity? She did not know. She trimmed them a little. The clippers sounded like chalk scratching awry. He shook himself away from her and went to sit in the living-room. "Women always go too far," he said.

He sat expectantly, his hands hanging limply between his knees. She was to make conversation. Suddenly, she was nauseatingly weary. "I've got to go to bed, John."

He made no move. Then she knew he had no place to stay. She thought crossly, let him sack out on the sofa, then remembered the fit of DT's he had when they let him stay last time. "How's the book business?" she asked.

"Not doing too well."

"Times are getting harder. Where do you live, now?" She did not want to be specific, she was beginning to feel sleepy and focussing would drive that away, but there was some final effort to be made with him.

"Nowhere, actually." There was a descent in pride if he did not bother to lie.

Wearily, she took Marvella's money out of her pocket. "That's all I can do, John. I can't have you to stay when Norman's away."

"You haven't found any books lately?"

"I can't take the three of them into the stores any more, they pull the bookshelves apart."

"I saw a red school reader that you'd like. I'll get it for you."

"No, buy yourself a roof, John. You're looking sick."

"You're a good woman, Minn."

"I'm sorry to push you into the night, John." For a second she hesitated, thinking yes — no. He watched her face and flinched, then. And lurched into the rain and the dark.

11

She was in her nightgown sitting on the chair in the bedroom, staring at the bed. It was a low bed, and the only way to get out of it without help these days was to roll out onto the floor, twisting her head awkwardly away from the bookcase. The extra mattress was another thing they would not get around to buying. She did not like to be in things she could not easily get out of.

Setting a bad example to the children, unwilling to sleep, unable to go without sleep. She hoped that tomorrow she would not have a hangover. Should sleep, must sleep. Cold now. House damp. Need a comforter.

Goddamn low bed, neither of us like it. I get into it too early for him, he lowers himself later after a hundred

111

despairing antique movies, thinking, no action. I feel him after he is snoring. Leonard Cohen on television, talking about staying up all night as a form of rebellion, right he is.

Five hours, six if lucky. Couch in the kitchen may be better. Harder, higher, no, I won't hear them when they wake. Can't put them outside tomorrow, swill of mud out in the back there. Eggs for breakfast. Scrambled. Flakey on the broom. God, let her come and say she'll fumigate. Could I get a lawyer? Anything kills bugs can also kill children. When he comes home I'll stand firm, I'll say, get me out of this house or I'll leave you. Then he'll look hurt, and I'll melt, I know.

No sound from the attic. Are they sleeping? Maybe I ought to check on them. Haven't been up for weeks except to capture a baby. No, not violate their privacy. Something I want to give them. Wish Richard would keep out of the kitchen, or be usable. Am mad as Alice: "Many hands make light work" and sweeping us all into a work bee. Compulsive worker, Alice. Ghastly cardigans she knit me: no taste in any department — poor Alice.

Funny seeing Sam again. He doesn't wear the bottoms of his trousers rolled, it's not the same person. Do they feel themselves calcifying?

Seeing everybody again. Now nobody will come for weeks. So little of the time I am lonely. Bad for the children, a too self-sufficient Mum. They have to observe normal social relations in order to have them.

But then, who wants normal social relations but me and the *Ladies Home Journal?* Best kids come out of crazy, cranky families. Pooh to bland environments. Betty standing outside the school watching what kids wear to spare her children agonies. Not the way to do it. Might never have left Godwin but for things like cousin Velma's bloomers. They'll have their agonies over us, hating our ways and their own names. Damn child-books and their forgetting parental pleasures. Give it a name YOU like to warble and to hell with it. Lafcadio?

People are funny. Reiner's health-group, nothing inside them. Low-definition vitality in spite of the trappings.

Versus Cal and his wearying personal hugeness. Have him around the house three days and go crazy. Five years old at heart and making everything into a story. Has me and Guinèvre right, though.

Lie down, old dog, give up the day, give up the night. John Colebrook's lying down, maybe underneath our steps. Lower yourself with the slow dignity of movement pertaining to pregnancy. Oh, I want to be quick again, dart like a dragon-fly. Never will be, suppose, now. Feel like a worn-out cart-horse.

Funny, imagery stuck in a dead world. Two pedlars do this neighbourhood pulling their own carts. They do not cry "Ragaboaaaaa . . ." There is still the bell of knives-to-grind, the popcorn steam-whistle. In Godwin, winter mornings, the street-ploughs came: men in striped tuques with wooden triangular ploughs and bells in their horses, celebrating snow's magic. Only once or twice a year there was enough snow for them. Then, suddenly, there was a kind of tractor . . .

Lie down, lie down now, you'll make it. Head on pillow, there.

I don't want to.

O, somebody come and cover me and mother me.

Rigid. Rigid till dawn when the babes awake, then right out. Like all the other nights. Telling yourself ego-stories until the conscience reels. How did I get to Whitsun weekend at Wheeler's End in England: coarse laughter as the bumpkin's daughter was pasted with her label: Miss Wheeler's End. Was asked to try to be Miss Petrolia once. I would have needed a strapless bathingsuit and knew better than to ask for it. Barbara Bennett won, who went on to the glory of *Miss Ontario Meatpackers Association*.

Stop. Just stop, there. Nights you come home from a party and talk his ear off. Can't shut you up to screw you. Cool it. Think of — well, water. Think of, if that's what water does to you, something, well, soothing. Recite something: The splendour falls on . . .

There is sweet music here that softer falls: that's a nice one. Don't get on to Alice's teeth when she said it. Alice couldn't help her teeth, do you think Old Man

113

Flintoft would have sent her to an orthodontist if there were any? Some people's teeth are like that. There are people whose jaws should never marry, they don't take that into consideration, their kids come out whistling.

Ben can hum. There is something remarkable about coming across a two-year-old humming. Hums and turns in circles on his bottom.

Wish Til had a talent. Perhaps no woman would notice hers.

Don't think of them. You've got all tomorrow. You can't *skip* tomorrow. If that's what you're hoping.

They fixed the doorbells, didn't they?

A sharp buzzing asininity of a sound, a handful of doorbells penetrating . . .

She put her arms around herself and thought, I won't answer it. But I won't sleep if I don't, and I want desperately to . . .

Some drunk. John. Oliver raping the air for Marvella. Cal, with a bright idea. Some friend of Speed's and Gary's, desperate. Norman, home unexpectedly without his keys. Oh, wouldnit . . .

She rolled out with difficulty, got up on her hands and knees and pulled from the end of her bed her housecoat. Then groped until she was standing, put it on herself. The bells went on ringing.

Without turning the lights on, she stumbled into the front room to look out the window. She stepped on a round toy and fell forward, rolled on the floor on her belly like a balancing clown toy, see-sawed on the foetus. So solid, she thought, and what if it hurts him. But he's got his cushion of water and what have I got? A bruised belly. Will I ever get out of this? Will it hurt us?

She got up by hauling on the rocking-horse, half-surprised that it was possible. The bells rang, shocking the night, another time. She peered shakily out, hanging on to the curtain. There were men's voices below, but the figures were shielded by the eavestrough.

114

Then she saw to the right, up the street, a cop car *couchant*. And someone dark stepped back and saw her, called out "Open up, we can see you."

Paranoia peering over the shoulder of honesty. No reason to be afraid. These are the nice men who bring lost children back and teach them school safety rules. Dreams of trial and error are self-justifying, an attempt to infuse drama, vision of a final victory over respectability. Nothing to fear, here.

And it would be something to be beaten physically, broken. No, not masochism: justification. It would be real, it would hurt and I would cry out, there would be marks on my skin, no one would help me. I would not fall back on being middle class, I swear it. The wounds would be external, visible. I would wear them like stigmata, and say to everyone, "Look what society has acted out."

Horsemen or locals? City police in that kind of yellow car. Blaze under the streetlight.

Look fellas, there's nobody here but me and a million kids and a billion cockroaches, it's late, come back in the morning. I'm for law-and-order too, you know, I spank my kids no matter what the books say. Go back from where you came from, I'm as big a pig as you are.

They rang again. Then they began to hammer on the door. She felt white and drained inside. She went downstairs to them, repeating to herself, if they aren't Horsemen, they can't come in without a warrant; if they haven't a warrant, they can't come and disturb respectable people. And if you live on Bute Place, you aren't respectable people. I am going to ache in the morning.

She caught herself at the bottom of the stairs with the sudden thought that she should waken the attic. But it was too late. They were banging on the inside door now, the bastards. She had visions of broken bluebirds. She opened it.

"Who do you want?" she asked, sticking her nose in the crack like a suspicious landlady.

"Police constable here," a firm voice said. Not limey, not Glasgow, the domestic leather-jacketed product.

115

"Mrs Williams here," she said as firmly. "Whom do you want?"

"I'm looking for Richard Potter."

"Well, look at a better hour."

"What do you mean, lady?"

"It's two o'clock in the morning."

"I've got his father with me. He's come to take him home to Napanee."

"Richard's from Kincardine."

"I'd like you to open up, Mrs Williams."

Then she remembered that she wasn't Mrs Williams, she was Mrs Burge. She grew afraid of herself, she knew she was slipping. She might have said Mrs Honeyman and never have known it. Only sure of the Mrs, not the rest. "Look," she said, "I'm not well, and . . ."

But they knew the vagaries of ancient doorways, and the door opened almost in her face, with speed, but also some kind of quick control.

The cop was very large, and made of rare roast beef. He was in uniform, he had his badge on, he did not look unsympathetic. His name was Ronnie Taunton and she had met him once with Norman, late in somebody's kitchen or in the back of the restaurant they used to hang out in, before they had children, when Norman was on the police beat. He and his buddies were entertaining the crowd with descriptions of what they did with old drunks, and it was not attractive.

I never saw anyone doing anything awful, she prayed to Gertrude, but I swear to God, Ma, I heard them saying they did. I've been radicalized.

She tried to look Ronnie in the eye. He half-recognised her — to the extent that he seemed to know he had seen her before — and shifted his gaze stolidly. The man with him wore brown, and a sharp-folded fedora over his sharp, foxy face. He might have been Richard's father, but he looked too withered. Poor Richard was the kind of boy of whom even the most liberal-minded said, "Put 'im in the army, do him a world of good" and she saw in this man's face what world, and decided that Richard could go on weeping in her teapot, bother or not.

116

"Have you got a warrant, Ronnie?"

Still, he didn't recognise her. Why should he? Years ago, some reporter's woman, edge of the crowd, women not something he noticed. And she had changed from a pretty girl to a pregnant squaw in four, five years. You didn't get any consideration unless you and your house were expensively fixed up.

Oh, they were good to you if you panicked over lost children, they were endlessly willing to tag cars in your driveway or drive you to hospitals, she had once shamelessly talked one out of a ticket by making eyes at him, they were not as implacable and fearsome as their reputation, why did she have to be afraid?

But Richard? Limp as a squirrel behind bars, without the energy to kill himself. Without also, though, enough life-love to keep him alive. They would be all he needed.

"Why do you want Richard?"

"I want him home," the brown man croaked.

"Why didn't you come by yourself?"

"I thought, these places . . ."

"How flattering of you."

"Mrs Williams . . ." Ronnie the cop was courteous, not however deferential.

I could put him in his place by telling him I'm Burge's wife, but what do I do about the Mrs Williams?

"You can come and see him in the morning," she said.

"Mrs Williams . . ." Ronnie put his big hand on her shoulder. He was very tall and had a chest so blue-shirted and comforting she could have sunk into it thinking, I'm home, home again. Instead, she twisted, as Ben had taught her to twist from a grip. Her eye fixed on the gun in his belt. The bloody Nazi.

He put one boot on the stair and nodded to the brown fox to follow him. She whispered, "Your warrant?" He shook his head and put a foot behind the first one.

She tackled him, flying, a hundred and seventy-five pounds of her, and the edge of the new kid against the edge of the stair, and the cop's boot wanting to kick and thank God not able or willing (Why should I be spared? she asked herself). And she tasted the blood of her own

tongue, first, and then saw his blood, where she had
scraped with her nails a carbuncle on the short-shorn neck
of him. She lay on him, fought him, pounded his back with
her fists in a flash of thunder, rammed her fists in his
kidneys, smelt the sweat on him, banged her head on his
back and sank her teeth through the serge of his jacket,
screaming, No, not in my house, no, authority, wet towels,
bums in the alleys, you cocks, and more that was obscen-
ity, like the time at camp swimming skinny and finding
that the counsellor chasing you in the dark was a stranger,
nothing to do with the place; alien, aggressive; lying under
the wet dock naked, beached, kicking and shouting words
she did not know she knew.

She heard serge rip. She tasted his blood. She stopped,
then.

The house was oddly quiet. She had spent her fury on
Ronnie Taunton's kidneys. She let him go. He flopped over
like a whale on the gritty stairs, looking up at her. She had
a great feeling of shame and a great feeling of victory. "I'll
say in court you hit me, if you charge me. Because Norm's
away and the children, the Children's Aid Society can't
have them."

"You're Burge's wife."

"I'm Mrs Williams to you."

He was panting. "You put up a good fight, lady."

"What're you arresting him for?"

"He's the kid's father."

"My fat fanny he is, in the bloody middle of the
night."

"Sure he is."

"You tried going up without a warrant. What kind of
people are you? You try again, Ronnie, I know which
bannisters are loose."

"This is some house, all right. What do you live down
here for?"

"None of your beeswax."

"We'll be back tomorrow. With a warrant."

"The kid wants his father."

"So?"

118

"So bring somebody who looks like his father."

He stared at her, but she could read nothing in his expression. Some look they taught him in cop-school, she decided. "The kid's not pushing and not doping," she said. "I've had worse kids in my attic. If it was hard drugs I wouldn't have cared, but poor Richard's not into anything more grown-up than glue-sniffing, and he doesn't buy plastic bags. It isn't hard drugs, is it?"

"That's our business, lady."

"You better take it somewhere else, then. Or are you going on up? Who do I call then, the cops or the night city editor?"

"We'll be back tomorrow." He got up stiffly and straightened his uniform tunic, brushed his backside. "You OK, now?"

"I guess so." She stood. She could. She tried to wipe something off her tongue, took it away from her lips with her fingers and discovered it was a flake of the bugger's skin. She felt sick, then.

The man in brown had not changed his expression. He was lynx-eyed, half-interested. He jerked his head towards the door, as if to escort Ronnie.

"Listen," she said, "I don't care if you charge me. If you feel you have to, you can charge me."

Ronnie stared at her. "Don't do it again. And don't think I won't tell your old man."

He stood in the doorway, very Western movie, gun on hip. "Let's get moving," he said to his podner. "Good-night," he said to Minn.

"Nobody goes upstairs in my house with a gun," she said. "And without a warrant. My father . . ."

"So long as you keep the law, lady." He went out, swinging his big legs from his hips, and the brown man trod uncertainly behind him, looking back at her for a moment, and muttered "Crazy people." They closed the doors behind them very quietly.

"We were good people," she said to herself from the steps, "we were good people. We never stole or swore or

119

drank or wore cheap shoes. We got up early, we went to church on Sunday. We were workers, we never committed excesses. We didn't touch ourselves or play with ourselves. We did our homework."

She cradled her baby and her belly in her big arms. She tried to strain a tear out. "What will you do without the Bible and Bill Shakespeare, pretty ones?"

But it was hurting, oh God, it was beginning to hurt now and there was no knowing if the pain was physical or psychic, because her belly was cramping, cramping meanly. In little short shoots, like fucking in your period, and paying for it after. Small bands of fear or taboo circulating like elastics. Not dilation. Nothing so large and satisfying. Mean little jabs of viciousness.

What were they doing here? Who did they think I was? Does everybody give in? Would I be ruined by a record for preventing a policeman from breaking the law?

Who pays them? What do they think they're upholding? They get so far away from the main thing, keeping some kind of civilisation going, and off into boondoggle. That's decadence. That's danger, Gertrude.

Damn little sharp shoots inside, I never meant to hit him. A piece of his skin — but he was all covered, sure he was, up to his ears in official blue cloth — in my mouth. I've tasted blood, now, and what good does it do?

Imagine the camps, the concentration camps.

A mean, ungiving sensation. Bamboo sprouts growing through. Could be a mushroom in there, given the house, the weather.

Time I had Louisa and was sluggish and they let me walk the corridors for exercise, and I saw the girl I shared the labour room with — young and cold and lonely — in the delivery room, whimpering on the table. White as paste and her stretch-marks vivid blue-purple, strapped there. More like a horse than the cow they compare us to, and the marks on her body, purple rivers. We had been together a moment before, flinging about our bodies uncomfortably, dancing, sometimes, beside the high beds, trying to reach an equilibrium. And she was frightened. She was going to tear open, she knew it. She had a woman doctor who flung away the cigarette I gave her, snarling "She's had her injection, you should know better," and made her climb up on the ironing-board stretcher by herself, still whimpering, and stalked into the delivery room beside her.

Then left her alone.

There wasn't anyone with her. I stood in the doorway, wondering. She was trussed like an animal, moaning. She was big, blowsy with her pregnancy; circled under the eyes. Beautiful thin blue-white skin, all marred and marked, now. About eighteen.

I went into the waiting-room to see Norman and say there was not after all going to be any business today, it had all gone away again. An accented lady said her daughter was in the delivery room, wasn't it a pity her son-in-law was working. One knew, then, that there was no son-in-law, that the girl was being punished.

Alone, and so cold there. Visitors say the rooms are over-warm, but you're cold, there.

I could have it here. I could go and get some newspapers and hunker against the wall on them the way Grantly Dick-Reid says, bracing my back. He tells you what to do on a beach, as an example: on the clean shingle, find something to brace your back on, some vagrant vertical, then squat, as the women of old did, then count, pant, control yourself.

I could do it. Sure, the hall's not clean enough but there's some kind of sterile power in newsprint. Squat, pant, eject, get it over with.

But not tonight. Tonight it would be a hostile act of excretion.

But why not? Do even elderly multiparas have no independence?

Them and their war-wounds, their emotional cruci-fixions. Don't know the ocean-rolls, the unbearable-bearable implosions. Short, sharp, then eased by the woozy sinking of the hypo into the epidural layer of the spine, and the pain going away and you grateful as a child brought out of a tantrum, smiling, saying your thank-you. Then, high on the epidural, talking. Oh, I talk on an epidural, and Mordie says, "Don't you want to see your baby delivered? I got you in the room with the mirror," and you look and see anus opening, like a red, red rose. Then hands, giblets: baby.

Then do it here, now. Feel, it's getting stronger. Twinge of twat. Medical students' anatomy books with moustaches on cunt. Brace yourself on the beach.

Pretend — Benny and Til are already pretending — pretend it's a beach, see, here, squat. Paper already on the floor, for snowboots. Old, open and turn over. Wonder if dilated? Feel. Be brave about it. Could put a teddy-bear in it's grown so wide, now, but has it, at the top, opened? Fancy a man facing furry corridors, first time into the bush. The quick brown cock shafts the hairy dog.

Magine having it on your own, here. Pulling it out raw into your own hands, biting the cord instead of a cop's bottom, could you? After screaming at kid mess could you face your own crap? The darkly inevitable connections that cheat us of air and fancy. Let it open, it isn't wooden, let it give, shunt life out. Emit that object, the valued and valueless child.

Life is cheap, now. Though we fail to admit it. Think of . . .

Dont't think of places. You are here.

What would Mother think?

It is an offence against the Criminal Code to give birth having failed to make prior and proper arrangements for the event.

So you wear the skin off your elbows on starched hospital sheets straining, prepared in the hospitals against grisly accidents. Morning after the storm: "Do you need a pill for your milk, dear?"

The hang of the gut, now. The slow swinging shift of the viscera.

Nothing is as socially acceptable as giving birth the first time. You are an initiate. After forty hours in the labour room if not always in labour: bonanza.

If he stayed away forever, we could manage. I might need a man, physically. I'd have to lose weight to get one.

I'd have to give more parties. Or maybe we could go back to Godwin. I could run a cultural counter-intelligence: "Mummy, what is God?"

"God is the first syllable of the name of an English social reformer who also wrote a good mystery novel I've never read."

There's room in that house. A row of beds would justify Annie's nursery. Myself in Willie's room. Gertrude dying grudgingly around us, Alice fussing over disorder. When they're in school I'll con Barney into giving me a job in his office. I can go evenings and talk to Lucy, if she lets me, though goodness she's cranky now. More like Mother than she and Gertrude admit. Last time she lectured me: giving yourself over to child-bearing and body-think, she said, and bodies think badly. Death in childbed seems to end every feminine revolution.

No, body can't think. The pains have stopped now. Shock reaction, suppose it was. Go to bed, now. You don't need to protest by having it in the hall. You'll never be a Dreikurs mother all-wise with the perfection of a perfect canteloupe: that went long ago. But you can struggle on if you get a little sleep.

What if they capture him, and he disappears with those other journalists? Can he steal stones along the Royal Way? Maybe he never made it to Nepal.

Night stretches and snaps ... had enough today. Could give birth to a cop chewing on a giant onion. Up, now. Feel around to make sure nothing's happened, then to bed. Girl at university had double-jointed elbows and periodically aborted herself. It took talent.

But the step's slippery. Blood? Mucus? Filthy stairs, hate sweeping them, dust, sand, slut's wool, germ-rife. Die in the muck, kids find me stark, staring, bag and child shivering, connected still, shrunken, congealed, hard as dried mushrooms. Wanting to die of captivity on winter afternoons, but not now, no, Lord, not now. Make me dead, but not yet, Lord. Puerperal fever, why we go to hospitals, why the draping, not nonsense. Proust's father, the great eipidemiologist. Goddamn Arts mind, Minn, get out of poetry into action.

123

Don't want to get up, don't want to . . .

Face it. Three kids up there, if he can't afford you, can Norman afford a housekeeper? Call the cop back, ask him to drive you to the hospital. He'll drop the charges if you tell him where to find the rubber sheet for the car. Brown man can babysit. Let them take Richard and Speed and Gary, someone will take them anyway. Get up, girl, get moving.

Can't get up, can't. Immobilized. Sitting on the stopper.

And was the bathtub clean when you got in it?

Can't get up. Needhelp, wanthelp, didn't ask to be . . .

Up, girl. And put the hall light on.

Needhelp. MARVELLAAAAAAAA.

She trolled the name into the night, the house echoed with it. She listened. One of the children moaned. Nothing else answered.

Nothing sleeps like the age of eighteen.

She pulled herself up on the bannister, feeling the curve and the coats of enamel that masked it, feeling the damp and the faint stickiness at the edges, rubbing her cheek against it. Then, cautiously, bent like an old woman, she moved down the one step and across the hall to press the light on.

She could have laughed then, she almost sat down again and laughed. But she knew what to do in this situation and she went off to do it. She had wet her pants. She went to the kitchen and brought back the wet-mop. Thinking, as the damp restored to the black-painted steps a clean artificial gleam, you crap when they hang you.

12

Then she was blanched and very still for a while. She sat down at the father's end of the dining room table and held her head in her hands. The room was chilly, but the smell of smoke was almost gone. She laid her cheek against the table and heard the furnace shudder on. It was like putting your face on the desk and listening to the gurgling of the stomach of the school.

Peaceful now; almost asleep. But something circled in her mind, one bird that would not come home to roost. She checked her obligations against her conscience, the door was locked, the windows were all shut, the only duty was to go to sleep, yet . . .

Norman's mum bore the two eldest in a sod house in Saskatchewan and cooked for the gandy-dancers in the summer, and now she's seventy and runs a book store. Her eyes dance with contempt when I complain. She had the other four after the big house went up, but then the bad times came. Norman doesn't remember being anything but happy there, they were better off than some of their neighbours, and his parents were good at managing what little they had. But one by one, the neighbours left. The school was closed. Ma Burge taught them at home until Polly, the youngest, got measles and went blind. They packed and sold, they'd had enough. They went to live with her sister in Vancouver. A month later, the father was killed in a traffic accident. She got work as a cleaning-woman and was glad to have it. The boys sold papers on streetcorners when they could get the job. Two of them went into the navy during the war and were lost at sea. Ma Burge still rises at six and sings while she works.

Then she remembered something and pushed herself up to fetch the mail from where she had hidden it this morning, when the children were flailing around her like a pack of young hounds and there was no hope of reading privately. She took the stack of envelopes from the top of the refrigerator and let the bills sift gently to the floor so that she remained holding Norman's letter gingerly.

She put off opening Norman's letters as she postponed opening the bills and the bank statement when she did not want reality to interfere with her attempts to maintain a poetic view of life. Sometimes she kept his letters for days without opening them. It was easier, it was nicer to file him on a mountaintop and forget about him while he was away, and in addition she had never been able to develop a satisfactory correspondence with him. She wrote to him awkwardly and unexpressively and his letters to her often seemed to be just more pieces of copy, nothing personal except obligatorily towards the end. Still, tonight . . . She went back to the table and decided to open it.

"Dear Heart," (he was given to quaintness when he felt emotional), "Tonight I went with a US infantry captain who has a Ph.D. from Wisconsin in philosophy and a passion for Busby Berkeley (no kidding, he knows every one of them frame by frame and wants to write a book on the guy if and when he ships home), to a tiny theatre in one of the rough quarters just out of range of the money-changers to see – guess what? – *Maria y Cristobal!* You were in good shape and I was homesick.

"There weren't any cuts that I noticed, so I got a chance to study the whole thing without commercials, if you don't count Arabic and Dutch titles at the bottom and Chinese up the side. French dialogue, it's a pity you didn't have a speaking part. I liked the way you stood looking wistful by the wall. It must have been hot. You had better boobs than the leading lady.

"It was good to see Aigues-Mortes again. I was intolerably reminded of walking the walls there, and the ferryman who came out of nowhere at Bac-le-Sauvage, and of the time you said the flamingoes over the Camargue looked like Canada geese flying backwards. But if you're praying to the old perfectionist, you'd better tell him there's a corner — just a corner — of a café umbrella showing beside the church in the scene where they parade Cristobal down the main drag. His mind must have been somewhere else. What irked me was that I couldn't remember whether Cinzano or Dubonnet umbrellas were the red ones. Do you?

"I seem to be doing such a good job here they have offered me another three months' tour. I pointed out to them that the insurance they pay for a man with four and three-quarter dependents must come too high. They agreed. They are now looking (slowly) for a free ride home for me. Tell Mordie I'll want you in good shape . . ."

Then there was something about the weather, something about things he had bought for the kids. She smoothed it out neatly on the table, taking care with the tatty corners, put her face on it, and, finally, slept.

13

Morning. Stars over. Light behind the curtains changing, shifting, green as celery. Outside, the big diesels breaking wind, the paper trains shunting farther off. Thwack against the loose front door goes *The Globe and Mail.*

Waking, and in the dining room. In Norman's green pyjamas pulled out of the laundry basket, not meeting in front. Chilly. Well slept, and upright on a hard chair.

Stiff. How the . . .? Last night. Don't think about it. Not until the Children's Aid comes for the kids. Give it a couple of weeks to settle in the cortex and make a flinchless memory. Don't phone anybody.

Bruised. What you get for beating up policemen. Setting an example. Where do you stand, girl?

Could have bitten his balls off. Never been so angry.

If they were really Nazis they would have fought back.

Fingernails broken. Wonder he didn't charge me. He won't come back today. Promises made after midnight are never kept.

Stand. Can. Good. No head-ache either. Need a bath. Pipes will wake the kids. Wash in the kitchen. Have a coffee.

Something fresh and light about the day. On three hours' sleep, I'm high and happy. Is that the lightening, the dropping? Mordie says his girls flock to the hospital the day the daffodils come out. So much for science. No, they all screw and bring their babies on.

When Norman comes home we'll open the Beaujolais, he'll make a *daube* with steak and a lot of garlic and good salt pork from the Hungarian and the dried orange peel. Then go up to the country and get a jack; first the anatomy lesson in the kitchen, then saddle of hare. We'll marinate pig to taste like boar, I'll cook it in sour cream after the children have gone to bed on bologny.

Since *Babar* has taught them to think that mushrooms are poisonous.

Get the juniper berries Tamblyn's, College and Spadina. They used to have a jar there. Juniper is Guinèvre. Jennifer, Juniper, Guinivere, gin: construed.

Give anything to be little like that, little, small, neat at the edges, deft. Able to work a vacuum cleaner without strangling in the tubes.

Mouth like the bottom of a birdcage. Ugly Canadian speech. We have to write plays in English and Irish accents here, the natives use their mouths so badly.

Coffee, cigarettes, newspaper. My drugs. Rotten world, always has been, only now we know it. Norman helping to spread the gloom around.

Best to read the obituaries. People have good names. The Cecils are going. A Barbara is 94. Don't usually put in how old they are any more, or much about them. Ads expensive, or undertakers hand out very short forms. *New York Times* is better; not so much the deaths, but the genealogies in the engagement notices. People here still think it's brassy to communicate. Gertrude hates the press.

Like people to die. At a decent age. Move over, make room for Burges. Knew those people, big connection from around Hespeler, four cousins at university with me. Maths and athletics. Sincere, plain, ex-Mennonite. Lieutenant-governor and money in there somewhere. Gran's gone at last.

Comics aren't what they were.

Faint bleats and mumblings from upstairs. Give the twins half an hour to clamber out of their cribs and unpin each others' pants.

Funny women last night. Looked like gilded insects, dragonflies. Sinister effect. Clothes are costumes. People are getting so theatrical you wonder what they're running away from. Norman and I are lucky; whatever you can say about our people, they were never dull.

Should do myself up more. Loathe plastic. Don't own anything non-mechanical made after 1928. Must try to adjust, be modern. *Il faut être absolument moderne . . .* We got that far, haven't progressed. Bad for the kids to grow up with art-deco fuddie-duddies. Elderly parents no good for teenagers.

Next year Louisa's locked into fourteen years of elementary education. Can't get over that, remember it too well: nineteen and rancid with yearning when you get to university. Will Shakespear was out working before sixteen, Mill was doing Latin at Weezie's age. Give her a reading lesson today. Only she won't accept it. Not going to be pushed into print.

Last night, the cop. Bang-bang you're dead. Where did the children learn it, down here with only me to play with and censored television? In the air, is it? Or in the psyche?

Someone's singing now. A high hum.

We call the moon The Lady Moon for them, and read them *The Snow Queen* when they'd rather have Dr Seuss, and celebrate the pagan festivals: Midsummer, Hallowe'en and the birth of the Corn King.

Louisa's learned to wink. She leers grotesquely. You'd think she had a wooden bum.

If this one's an Annie?

Cross that bridge when you come to it.

I won't be able to handle them on three hours' sleep. Doze in a chair outside the playroom gate and toss them cookies? What do we pay the pedodontist for? Call Doris in. What'd I do with Marvella's money? Oh, God!

Somewhere we lived once a queer paraded a pregnant dachshund in front of the house every night. Its poor tits scratching against the sidewalk, himself mincing ahead with that waggle of the bum they do, the bitch tottering behind; women in doorways wincing and glowering at the two of them.

London. About the same time Ivan Dennison had the job that saved our lives. He had to go from door to door in a box-shaped green costume and say "I'm the Fairy Snow-Man." He loved it. Every fortieth housewife who had a box of the goddamn detergent on the shelf got a five-pound note. The newspaper strike was on. I bought a lot of Fairy Snow and when he got to thirty-nine he'd take a taxi to us. There'd be enough over from the rent for kippers and Woodpecker cider for lunch and by the time he was fired he had a part at the Royal Court and the strike was over.

Poor spavined dog.

Maybe I'll turf Marvella out and rent the gables to a student. She can move from room to room with the weather. It would be an empire up there. We never had anything half that good in London. If Norman wants to make love to her, let him. I'll be able to sleep again.

I think he's faithful. I wouldn't be.

The day is spotted with light, freckled, vair, variegated. And all the children are different.

After the kids are all in school the dreary mums bloom again. They get new clothes and sprint from job to job singing. It works until they collide with paranoid teenagers and fall back mortally wounded. They need to be stronger, like Gertrude, like Norman's mother. Country stock, militant in its one desire, not to be thought Irish.

Can't imagine getting anywhere on time now. Never did before. Suppose getting them up for school is practice. All the clothes you used to have to go to work in. Girdles and stockings. Smart little black suits. And gloves. Even me.

Wake on a fresh, high-pressure morning like this, and the newspaper world's unbelievable. Frittering and fretting and nothing about first causes except from revolutionaries.

The kids have to fight us. We fight them. Need the tension. To extract from them the requisites of a civilisation we can't believe in.

We clutch each other in the dark and say, "It's going to be all right." It isn't, we hope, but words are comforting.

The devil damn thee black, thou cream-faced history.

And the kids are pigs and life is a great big truffle field.

I cry easily; my only profundity is "moo". I lie twitching for my master and who is he? I am ready for knives or scissors or forceps or Norman.

I try to forget wars and fevers; they're stuffed up in there with the foetus. An animalculum that claims to be humanoid. I hope it is.

Whatever happens, the universe will roll on somehow. It's big enough to do without us, there's a comfort. The tides will ebb and flow, the moon rise even if she isn't cheese or snow. *Das ewig Weibliche* will whip us from her dog-cart. *Das ewig Maennliche* will slog across the moor.

There will be war and murder and long winters and hot summers. You will have to have strong legs.

We will sit in a circle longing for the lights of Moscow. We will bite each other's fingers out of boredom, to see the blood. We will continue to clean our houses. We will make artifacts.

And the morning will come, and so will the night again. Won't it?